EL FLAMINGO

NICK DAVIES

YBK Publishers   New York

El Flamingo
Copyright © 2023 by Nick Davies

YBK Publishers, Inc.
39 Crosby Street
New York, NY 10013

ISBN: 978-1-936411-84-9

Library of Congress Cataloging-in-Publication Data

Names: Davies, Nick, 1992- author.
Title: El Flamingo / Nick Davies.
Description: New York : YBK Publishers, [2022]
Identifiers: LCCN 2022052915 | ISBN 9781936411849 (paperback)
Subjects: | LCGFT: Novels. | Thrillers (Fiction).
Classification: LCC PS3604.A95385 F53 2022 | DDC 813.6--dc23
LC record available at https://lccn.loc.gov/2022052915

Cover illustration by Vincenzo Ingenito

Manufactured in the United States of America
for distribution in North and South America
or in the United Kingdom or Australia
when distributed elsewhere.

For more information, visit
www.ybkpublishers.com

Contents

For the lost dreamers....

1

I looked at the worm keeled over at the bottom of a cheap mezcal and felt I could relate. He was the only one around with as little to lose.

Earlier that day, I'd quit acting for good and left Los Angeles. I'd crammed my belongings into my three-wheeled suitcase and forced my way onto the first flight out of LAX to Mexico. From there, I'd boarded a jam-packed bus that took me on a ninety-minute ride and dropped me off at a small tourist town somewhere down the Pacific coast. Playa del *something*-or-other. It had all the usuals—palm trees, cheap resorts, and a hundred-and-one taco stands—the failsafe bait of Western escapism. Any other day, I would say I was different, not just another lost goat in the common herd, but an *individual* capable of magnificent feats, but today, I was done lying.

I'd stepped off the bus and fought through a battalion of street hustlers selling everything from sombreros to women, to class-A narcotics. I'd resisted the urge to smash them out of the way with the three-wheeled suitcase, but only because it was so damn heavy.

Once clear of the initial madness, I arrived at my hotel, *Princesa's Paradise*. It cost twenty-five bucks a night and looked nothing like its online photos, but that's to be expected. Its pink pillars were chipped and faded, and for several minutes the reception desk appeared to be all but abandoned. Eventually, an overworked *señora* checked me into my room which featured little but a creaky queen bed, a cactus in the corner, and a bible in the bottom drawer. It was far from fit for a princess, but on the bright side, breakfast was included. You gotta be grateful for the little things.

After dropping my luggage, I changed shirts, put on my flip-flops, and headed back out. I hiked far and away from the touristy shit storm until, at last, I wound up here, a deserted little beachside bar, the kind where you could sip until sundown and forget your existence. Bottomless filter coffee had taken me as far as it could, so under the shade of the tiki-hut roof, I ordered a drink.

"A double shot of your cheapest mezcal," I said with as much pride as I could muster. "*Por favor.*"

My bartender had dark hair, tattoos, and eyes that didn't care. Around her neck was a skull pendant that stared my way and told me I was a dead-man-drinking. She pulled a half-empty bottle from the shelf, the same one that contained the dead, lonely worm.

"What's with the worm?" I asked.

She lethargically explained that its original purpose was to flavor the mezcal, but it had since become more of a novelty, a stamp of authenticity in the eyes of out-of-town gringos heading south of the border to drown their sorrows. She raised an eyebrow, then turned away, confirming what I'd expected. Worse than a failure, I was a cliché: Lou Galloway, a thirty-five-year-old dreamer in a pair of faded jeans and a cheap Hawaiian shirt. To hell with the lime and salt. I tossed it back neat, then ordered another.

A sand and sea-salt breeze tango'd around me, which helped to cool the tropical swelter. With not another soul around, I at least had the view to myself, the rosé pink of a dying sunset, shining on waves that washed ashore like ticks of a clock.

So why the one-way ticket to Mexico?

Well, like any actor this far south of southern California, things hadn't gone according to plan. I could rattle off tales of Hollywood heartbreak, just like every scorned dreamer to be chewed up and spat out by L.A., but I won't. I could tell you how no one cares what's real anymore; how all they want is white-toothed frauds and spray-tanned clones, it-boy actors there not for the craft, but for the parties. I could tell of the thousand times I bared my soul to a panel of stone-faced producers who never saw me as anything more than a skeleton of mediocrity; a cheap, smoldering headshot who walked in the room and gave them forgettable.

I could warn you not to be hypnotized by the sepia filtering the city like an old-time movie, a feeling in the air like you're *supposed* to be there because that kind of California glow could only light a path to glory. Don't be fooled. It might as well be dusty tints on a pair of third-hand shades. L.A.'s no city of dreams, it's just the world's biggest casino. It'll take your money, your time, and your very last *damn*. Then, it'll take your soul.

Three days ago, in a last straw of sorts, I'd received a phone call. I was put *on hold* for a big-time role, in a big-time flick, for a big-time studio. *On hold* is where you're down to the final two, and it's either you or the other guy. I'd prepped like a madman and nailed the hell out of the audition. With high hopes, I'd thought I might have finally found the all-elusive big break, the one that seems to never arrive.

But, this morning I'd received another call: lo and behold, they'd gone with the other guy. The producers felt he was just a little more "authentic."

Authentic? They wouldn't know authentic if it waltzed on over and kicked them in the shins.

Next to me on the bus ride in was a woman from Texas about as wide as Texas. I'd given her a look that said I wasn't open to conversation, but she'd blabbered on anyway. She said her name was Barb, short for Barbara, and she'd come down here to look for divine intervention. *"Just because I ain't been to church in*

nine years don't mean I ain't a church girl." She took
all kinds of pleasure in giving me a lifetime worth of
travel advice on Latin America.

"Stick to the tourist areas, *amigo*. No backstreets.
They can't get ya there."

They. People always talk about "they." Pisses me off.

"Mark my words," she went on. "On the life of my
bed-ridden momma, this whole Latin world is the most
beautiful thing you'll ever see in your lazy old life, but
there are two things you gotta be wary of. Dengue, and
the C-word."

"Dengue?"

"That's right. A mosquito you'll never even see will
sneak up on you and bite you in the ass. Takes about
a week for the symptoms to kick in. Then you'll get so
nauseous your brain swells up and you'll die a slow
death over ten to fourteen days, asking yourself if that
seaside margarita was really all worth it."

"Jesus Christ."

"I know. Then there's the *C-word...*"

"The C-word?"

She'd made a big deal of looking all around, then
leaned in close. "Corruption, *amigo*. It's everywhere.
Bad men with blood money in hand."

I'd heard it all before. People always talked about
Latin America as a God-forsaken land of bullets and
blood, but I paid it no mind. You gotta understand that
Mexico couldn't hurt me. No narco or dead-eyed *sicario*
could do anything the big shots of L.A. hadn't done
already.

Dengue, on the other hand...well, that really was a
concern.

I went to order another round when, seemingly from
nowhere, appeared the silhouette of a man sitting right
beside me, his face obscured by the glare of the sun. He
pulled a wad of cash from his shirt pocket, peeled off a
note, and placed it on the counter.

"Good thing there's a little mezcal left," he said. *"Un doble. Por favor."*

It was a voice of gravel and time that rang out like the first spoken lines in a lonely show, way Off-Broadway.

I looked a little closer.

The stranger had a hell of a style—a duet of light pink and chocolate brown. Pink linen shirt, the sleeves rolled up to reveal the forearms of a lean wrestler. Creaseless brown slacks. Shined leather boots. Aviator shades, tinted just enough to conceal his eyes. A brown fedora sat atop his head and tucked into the band was a feather. A faded *pink* feather, partially illuminated by the sunset glow. I imagined that, once upon a time, it might've fallen from the wing of a majestic flamingo.

"Hell of a sunset," said the stranger.

"Sure on its way down," I replied.

"It saved my life once. A long time ago."

"What did?"

"The sunset."

I looked away. You let some people start, and they'll never shut up. "Sounds like a long story."

"It ain't short."

He gazed at the bottle of mezcal with a regretful shake of his head. "Damn shame about that worm."

"How so?"

"If he hadn't been drowned in mezcal, he would have grown to become a *mariposa*."

"A *mariposa*?"

"A butterfly of the night."

It was just like I suspected. The dead worm, stripped of his destiny, robbed of his chance to fly into the night as his best self. As a *mariposa*. And me, the greatest actor never known, cast out by the land where dreams were meant to come true. That damn worm and I were one and the same.

Finally, the stranger turned my way and looked me

over. For a moment, he appeared to recognize me from some distant time and place that he couldn't quite recall.

"What do you say we make a toast?" he asked.

"To what?"

"To the worm."

I shrugged. "Sure. What the hell."

Another meaningless exchange of small talk between two drifters who'd found themselves at the same tiki bar at the same point in time. At least, that's how it appeared.

"To the worm beneath the mezcal," said the stranger. "Whose *mariposa* we never saw."

We raised our glasses and said *salud* as the sun continued west.

2

A shift in the light stole the shadows from the stranger's face. I'd say he was in his early forties. He had a grey-speckled beard as if he'd come in from a snowstorm, and the kind of jaw that, if you were to give it your best right hook at point-blank range, you'd only break a couple of fingers. And he was still, about as still as I'd ever seen anyone.

"What brings you to Mexico?" he asked.

"I didn't want to be who I was anymore. Had to hit the road."

"Mexico has that appeal. It'll let you escape. At least for a while."

"I'd rather not get into it."

"Sure," he said, "but out of curiosity, who were you?"

I couldn't comprehend why he gave a damn, but I indulged him anyhow. "I used to be an actor."

"Used to be?"

"Things changed."

"What changed?"

"Let's just say I reached a fork in the road."

"I see. And where does that leave you today?"

I gulped the mezcal and slammed the glass on the bar top. "As another guy in Mexico with shit-all to lose."

We let that breathe for a while, both of us watching the final rays of life from the runaway fireball.

After a time, I felt bad for snapping at the guy, so I summoned the energy to ask what brought *him* to Mexico.

"It would only bore you."

"C'mon. You know my story. Level with me."

He was silent for a spell, then said, "Typesetting."

"Sorry?"

"Typesetting. I sell equipment crucial and related to typesetting."

"If you don't mind me asking, what the hell is that?"

7

"The composition of text by means of arranging physical types or their digital equivalents. That's the dictionary definition."

A cover for shady dealings, if there ever was one, I thought. "Well, thanks for clearing that up. So, you sell typesetting."

"And related equipment."

"In Mexico…"

"Mexico and beyond. All through the Americas. It's where the demand is highest."

"Who woulda thought."

He removed his fedora and set it down on the bar top, revealing short brown hair combed in a way that was more for tidiness than a slick appearance. Sitting between us, the feather curved upward, a fluorescent question mark in the gathering twilight.

"An actor," he said. "I've always liked actors."

"And why's that?"

"They're dream-chasers. Something the world needs."

I said nothing.

"You got a name, *amigo*?"

"Lou," I said. "Lou Galloway."

"Sounds like you're pondering the meaning of your existence, Lou Galloway."

"That's one way to put it."

"I've been doing some of that myself lately," he continued. "You ever been in love, Lou?"

Now don't get me wrong, I'm a hopeless romantic. I had my fair share of chances, taken my shots, but in the end, they'd all come to nothing. I'd come to terms with the possibility of living out the rest of my days as a lone wolf. I couldn't say I'd found love, much less *fallen* into it.

"I'm not sure I know what love is," I said.

"You will if you're lucky, Lou. You're still young. At least for a little while."

"That's very reassuring."

He breathed out slowly, as if pushing through the weight of regret. "I've been in love with the same woman for as long as I can remember."

"Then maybe you should be watching the sunset with her," I said, "instead of with some has-been actor. Maybe you should get outta this bar and go win the woman back."

He peered straight at me, and I wasn't sure if he was going to hit me or hug me.

"You know, I've been thinking the same thing." He downed the rest of his glass with a grin. "You're alright, Lou."

He ordered another round for both of us, so I guess he was alright too. The hum of the town behind us had faded, replaced by the gentle howl of the ocean breeze.

I'd been trying to place the guy's accent. American? No. More American-ish, the way accents are when you've been in and out of foreign lands for a very long time.

The man turned back to me. "When was your last role, Lou?"

There it was, every failed actor's most dreaded question. I thought back to the last role, the last *real* role that truly meant something. It was years ago. I'd played a young version of *Don Quixote de La Mancha* in a one-act spin-off, shambolic and unpaid, directed by some mad old enthusiast at a dusty, hole-in-the-wall theatre in some forgotten part of L.A. It was a speculative work, centered around what shaped Quixote's mind as a young man that led to the famed pursuits of his older age. On opening night, only a handful of people had showed—lonely L.A. hearts with nothing better to do on a Tuesday night.

For what it's worth, they said I was brilliant. Some even claimed they were moved to tears, but you never know if they're just saying that. According to them, I was well cast. Of course I was. It's said that Don Quixote was the greatest fool in all of literature. The old man who set off on valiant adventures, determined to right the world's wrongs and preserve the very last of endangered chivalry, but whom the world saw as nothing more than a delusional eccentric, no different to most actors.

But I always saw Don Quixote as a symbol of the lost dreamer, an aging everyman who felt it was never too late to be his best self, to achieve the impossible, to ride into the world, seek out its villains, and accost them on sight; a moral soldier in his runaway mind. I never saw him as a fool, but maybe I'd missed the point.

"It's been a while," I muttered.

"Is that why you quit? You spent your life waiting for that one role that never came?"

"Something like that."

He twirled his shot glass in his hand, gazing at it, like it was a tiny globe that could take him anywhere, so long as he just imagined. I looked down the coast at the infinite stretch of white sand that eventually led to South America. About a mile or so away, a bonfire burned, sending a river of smoke into the sky.

"What if that one great role was right around the corner?" asked the stranger. "What if you quit on your dreams just a little too soon?"

"It doesn't matter anymore. I'm outta time. I'm done with the gamble of it all."

"Was it a gamble or an investment?"

"Gamble. Investment. Call it what you like. Either way, I played my hand, and I lost."

"Loss is inevitable, whichever road we choose. The secret is finding the ace."

"Yeah, well. What if you don't have an ace?"

"Sometimes you don't have to *have* an ace to *play* an ace."

"You use that metaphor when you sell typesetting?"

"Closes every time," he said with a wink.

In the distance, the bonfire flared, like a drunken reveler had tossed in a splash of rum to see it soar, unwilling to let the flames burn out.

The stranger asked the extent of my Spanish. I knew a few *palabras* and could understand the gist of general conversation, thanks to the current of Latin culture that'd flowed through southern California.

I shrugged. "Somewhere between *un poco y suficiente.*"

"*Muy bien.* Would you say it was enough to…get by?"

"Sure. Why not?"

The corner of his lip curled into a smile. "Well, Lou Galloway. I just might have something for you."

"Listen, I'm not looking to sell typesetting if that's where you're going with this."

Before I could get a straight answer on what the hell he meant by *something*, he abruptly stood. "I gotta shoot to the gents. Watch my hat, will ya, Lou?"

"Sure."

Before heading off, he said, "It's knowing you'd take a bullet for them, at any given moment."

"What is?"

He grinned, but didn't answer, then strolled away onto the sandy trail that led back to town. I noticed he walked right on past the sign for the *baños.*

"Wrong way!" I called.

If he'd heard, he'd ignored me, staying his course until he was out of sight.

I figured he'd realize soon enough and return for his fedora and one last round of mezcal. I started to give in to the tipsiness and closed my eyes. I must have dozed off, because by the time I opened them again, night had fallen. The bartender was gone, the mezcal packed away, and the bonfire had burned out. Sure enough, there was no sign of the man who sold typesetting.

Maybe he was drunker than he'd appeared and had wandered off into the night. Maybe I'd never see him again. Regardless, I was alone under the Pacific stars with nothing but an ocean between me and Timbuktu.

Still resting on the bar top was the fedora, traced by the moon's glow, as if under a spotlight on an empty stage.

I ran two fingers up the curve of the feather, and for a moment, I could swear it was speaking to me, hinting that it was waiting for someone. That it was *asking* to be worn. It may sound *loco*, but bear in mind, I'd had a lot of mezcal. Carefully, I placed the fedora on my head.

It was a perfect fit.

I tilted the brim down and a wave of nostalgia came over me, transporting me back to a time when I was just a young actor playing in the shadows of an old prop room, exploring the possibility of seeing the world through the eyes of another.

I walked to the shoreline to take a final look at the starlit horizon. In the calm water, my shimmering silhouette stood before me, a lone figure in another man's fedora. For a moment, Lou Galloway was a thing of the past, and, since the man who sold typesetting had disappeared, there was no one left in the world who knew where I was. I could have been anybody. In a drunken mumble, I addressed the fraudulent silhouette.

"Who the hell do you think you are?"

Before he could answer, a wave rolled in and washed him away.

There was nothing to do except call it a night, to return to my room at *Princesa's Paradise* and dream about breakfast. With the fedora still on, I started back toward the town, heading into the dark of the Mexican night.

3

I made my way through the dunes and onto the frac-
tured concrete as the sweep of the shoreline waves
grew distant. Balance was a struggle in my tipsy state;
my blurred vision helped little by the flicker of broken
streetlights.

I staggered past deserted cafés, bars, and restaurants. In a few hours, they'd be boiling up the first pots
of coffee and serving up *huevos rancheros* and *chilaquiles*, but for now, they'd all but closed down. It seemed
I was the last man alive in a Latin ghost town.

My phone vibrated in my pocket. I'd forgotten all
about it since I got to Mexico. There was only one person
in the world who would want to get hold of me on my L.A.
number—my agent, Tommy Blue. I answered the call.

"Tommy. What do you want?"

"Galloway!" he yelled through scratchy reception.
"Been trying to get a hold of ya for hours. Where the
hell are ya?"

Tommy was an Italian American salesman who quit
his job pushing used cars in the mid-eighties and drove
from New York to L.A. to represent actors. While he
was short of any major success stories, you couldn't
question his heart. No matter how bad things got,
when the deals broke down and the leads disappeared,
he never stopped thinking that our big-time days were
right around the corner. You gotta admire that.

"Mexico, Tommy. Alright? I'm in fuckin' Mexico."

"Mexico? Christ on a bike. Listen. I get it. Ya think
I don't get it, but I *do* get it. We took a little hit back
there and now you think you're out for the goddamn
count. Okay, so you gotta get away. Clear ya head.
Fine! Drink tequila, eat some tacos, get a dulce tan,
shack up with a local *señorita*, do whatever the hell
you gotta do. But you're comin' back to L.A. You're my
best client."

"I'm your only client."

"Watch your mouth!"

"And I'm never coming back to L.A."

"That's a pile of horseshit. Listen. Stick to tourist areas. No backstreets. The bad guys can't get ya' there."

Why did people keep saying that?

"No backstreets. Got it."

"Great. Now go get your dick wet, and I'll see ya' back in L.A."

"No, you won't."

"Hanging up now."

The line went dead.

Ahead, a pair of headlights flicked on. I squinted at the red and blue strobes of a *Policia* car easing closer and slowing to a halt. The doors opened. Two pairs of black boots thudded onto the pavement and strolled toward me in no kind of hurry. Barb from the bus ride had warned me about the cops down here. Said they had a reputation for arresting you for whatever the hell they felt like, unless you pony up a few thousand pesos for their back-pocket trust fund. Either that or enjoy thirty-six hours in a Mexican jail cell, all-expenses-paid. She added that a guy like me wouldn't do well in there. I stood up straight and tried to look as sober as possible. *Smile. Build a rapport. Just another drunk gringo, lost and confused in Mexico. Lo siento!*

I looked at the one who'd stepped from the passenger side, most likely the senior of the two. The alpha always makes the rookie drive, if going by the movies.

"*Buenas noches* office—"

"*Silencio*," said the alpha.

He had a double chin and a pair of eyes that were miles apart. The junior, who was twice as young but just as ugly, stood back. Maybe this was some kind of demonstration: Lou Galloway, Exhibit A in "*How to Shakedown a Gringo, 101.*"

"*Americano*, huh?" asked the alpha.

"*Sí. Americano.*"

"Don't speak Spanish," he said. "It's embarrassing."

"I'm sorry."

"Don't say sorry."

"Then I'll just say nothing."

"What kind of a fucking hat is that?"

"Believe it or not, it isn't mine."

"But it suits you so well, *pendejo*," sneered the junior. *Pendejo* means asshole. I know because I've been called one before.

"I.D.!" growled the alpha.

I pulled my I.D. from my wallet and handed it to him. He inspected it so closely, I could swear he was sniffing it.

"Lou Galloway. Sounds like an idiot."

Well, that was just mean.

He asked for *dinero*. I told him whatever was left in the wallet. He made a show of sifting through its dusty contents, only to come away with nothing.

"*Nada.* A *gringo* with *no dinero.*"

The two cops exchanged wide, gormless grins. It seemed my predicament was the highlight of their day. Maybe if I'd been sober, I would've held my tongue; acted with more caution; said the right things; defused the situation. But I'd lost the will to care anymore. Frankly, my dear, I just didn't give a damn.

"I can't decide," I announced.

The alpha stepped forward. "Can't decide what?"

"Which one of you two is uglier."

Their smiles flattened. "*Perdón, pendejo?*"

"Don't get me wrong. Both of you are *just* hideous. But trying to choose is like splitting hairs. So how about this? You're both just as ugly as each other. It's a good, old-fashioned draw. You're both just the ugliest sons-of-bitches I've ever had the bad luck of laying eyes on. Happy?"

The alpha grabbed me by my collar and drove me

smack-bang into the concrete wall. "You know what happens to *gringos* in prison down here?"

I could already feel a bruise forming on my lower back. The blow had taken the wind out of me, but I had just enough left for another witticism.

"A spate of romantic encounters, I'm guessing."

The alpha nodded to the junior like they'd done this a hundred times. He drew out a long, dark baton that resembled a nightmarish sex toy. He lowered his gaze to my crotch. I immediately regretted the wisecrack.

"Listen, fellas, I may have gotten a little carried away—"

"Shut up!"

The junior arched the baton back, ready to swing, when a startling shout rang out from down the street.

"*¡DETENTE!*"

STOP!

The three of us turned to see a short, portly figure struggling out of a black vehicle that just about took up half the street, the engine idling like the growl of a wild animal. The figure marched out of the shadows and stopped in front of the alpha. "Release this man," he ordered.

He looked about fifty, with a receding hairline and a moustache about as thick as his waistline. Peculiarly, he was dressed to the nines in a full tuxedo, bow tie, tails, and all.

"*Quién eres tú?*" asked the alpha.

The Tux cleared his throat. "Who *I* am is not important. What matters is who I *work* for."

The alpha glanced at the luxury car from which Tuxedo Man had arrived. A Rolls Royce Phantom.

"Well, who do you work for?"

The Tux beckoned him closer and whispered in his ear. The alpha's eyes just about popped onto the sidewalk. White-faced, he said, "*Señor*, I offer my apologies. I had no idea who you are."

Before I could ask who the hell he thought I was, the two cops hurried to their car and sped away, leaving The Tux and me alone on the empty street.

Who was this man? And why had he been inclined to keep me out of jail with nothing but the simple uttering of his boss's name? At the very least, I owed the guy a hefty *gracias*.

"*Señor*," I said. "*Muchas gracias* for...whatever the hell just happened."

"No, *señor*. *Muchas gracias* to *you*. For being here."

"Sorry?"

The Tux vigorously shook my hand, the sweat of his palms transferring to mine. "My name is Arturo. Apologies for my late arrival."

"Nice to meet you. My name is—"

"I know who you are, *señor*, and let me say, it is an honor."

He still hadn't let go of my hand. "An honor?"

"*Si, señor*. I am a huge fan of your work."

A huge fan of my work? How drunk was I?

Arturo escorted me to the Phantom. It had suicide doors, tinted windows, and the signature ornament of a woman, the Spirit of Ecstasy, bowing over the silver grill.

"*Vamos, señor*," said Arturo, pulling open the rear passenger door. I stepped back.

"*Vamos*? To where?"

Arturo's wide grin spread across his sweaty face. "To the fiesta, of course."

"The fiesta?"

"In accordance with the agreed arrangements."

"The agreed arrangements. Of course."

I thought I should really come clean, but damn, it felt good to be treated like I was somebody, if only for a moment.

Arturo offered a calm smile, then said, "Time is of the essence."

I couldn't consider the offer, could I? It would be audaciously unwise. Alone in a dangerous country with some unknown gentleman offering to take me to some party at an undisclosed location. It would take a madman to accept. But, the thing is, sanity had gotten me nowhere. I'd skulked down to Mexico to *forget* the world. Maybe this was fate trying to tell me something? The friendly insistence of this Arturo made it seem like the natural next step. I didn't want to disappoint him, not after he just saved my ass from a baton to the balls. I owed him. A judgment call was in order.

"You're right, Arturo. Time *is* of the essence."

I got into the Phantom.

As we drove away from the coastline, I recalled a detail from earlier in the night. It was the look on the face of the man who sold typesetting. I couldn't help but feel there had been some kind of subtextual exchange that may have gone over my head. Something in his eyes that had said we'd come to an agreement. An *understanding*. But about what, exactly?

Had I shaken hands with God? Or done a deal with the Devil?

4

Someone once told me, when you don't know what to say, say nothing. So was to be my plan, at least until I came into more information. Mainly, who exactly had I been mistaken for, and where the hell I was going. For the moment, I would stay silent and kick back in the comfortable leather seats of the Phantom.

Arturo drove cautiously, one eye on the road, the other in the rearview. We rolled through intersections and crept through red lights, never coming to a complete stop.

We passed beat-up bars and small adobe casas on the outskirts of town before hitting the straightaway stretch of the desert highway. Soon enough, we were enclosed by a dome of darkness, leaving little to see except the rutted asphalt of the road ahead.

Arturo met my eyes in the rearview mirror. "¿Música, señor?"

"Sure. *Música* would be good. *Muchas gracias.*"

He hit a button, and a voice began to sing over the riff of a Spanish guitar. It was low and husky and carried the rage of a woman scorned—heartbroken.

Arturo shook his head to himself. "Aha, *Señor.* How could I forget?"

He pushed another button and my armrest opened to reveal a miniature liquor cabinet containing a single bottle of whiskey. Etched into the glass was *"Envejecido 60 años."*

Aged sixty years. An upgrade from the tiki-bar mezcal, to say the least.

Beside the bottle was a polished whiskey glass with a message engraved on the side: *El Flamingo, Salud.*

"A gift for you, *señor*," said Arturo. "From the *jefe.*"

The jefe? The same *jefe* whose name had saved me from the corrupt Mexican state police? More importantly...*El Flamingo?*

19

I remembered the fedora, the one that sat atop my goddamn head. Like an idiot, I'd forgotten all about it. So Arturo must have been there to collect a guy in a feathered fedora, the hat being some kind of identifying accessory. This meant the guy he'd been looking for was the man who sold typesetting. Or *claimed* he sold typesetting, apparently known to his associates as *El Flamingo*.

El Flamingo...Jesus. It sounded like some kind of legendary guitarist or a world-renowned dancer. He sure as shit hadn't looked like the kind of guy to float around a ballroom, but there you go.

A cold sweat broke out on the back of my neck. What was to be expected of me?

Calm yourself, Galloway. Panicking will get you nowhere. I poured myself a shot of the sixty-year-old whiskey. The taste was rich in caramel and heavy in smoke, and it helped me to relax and formulate a plan.

When we arrived at the fiesta, I would simply own up. I'd say that there'd been a mistake. I'd underestimated the strength of the mezcal and had mistaken Arturo for my Uber driver. A classic mix-up that could happen to anyone. They would put it down to the silly ways of the *gringo* and laugh off the whole thing. Hell, they might even let me keep the whiskey. Everything was going to be okay. No one would expect me to dance, would they?

Arturo's voice brought me from my introspection.

"Deep thoughts, my friend?"

I recalled the words of the man who sold typesetting. "Just pondering the meaning of my existence."

"Ahh. The complicated mind of an American."

"Sorry?"

"*Nada, señor.*"

We submerged into the shadow of a mountain range. Arturo dropped a gear, then we began to climb a steep, winding trail, deep into the kind of terrain that keeps secrets from the outside world.

About a mile or so ahead appeared a light, a single sign of life in the dead of night. As we neared, the light grew broader until I doubted what I saw before me—a *mansion*.

More so, a Spanish-style hacienda of antique-white stone, guarded by spiked gates, like it might have been home to a Latin King in the 1700s. To encounter such a sight so late into the night, so deep into the desert, was extraordinary.

We approached the front gates, where a man in a black suit stepped out from a security booth. He had the kind of eyes that suspected everyone. In his hand was an assault rifle. My chest tightened. I'd seen armed men at airports and train stations before, but those guys had uniforms and government I.D.s.

Arturo buzzed the window down. The guard crouched and whispered something to Arturo, who whispered back. The guard gave me a look of what seemed like profound respect. Maybe even fear.

Before I could say something to put the guy at ease, he bowed his head and hurried back to his booth to allow us inside.

We eased up a long driveway lit by tall lamps, bordered by rose bushes and trimmed green lawns, edging closer to the magnificent palace. Stone pillars stood guard beside double-wood doors, and a water fountain made for one hell of a roundabout.

A parking valet awaited the car.

I stepped out of the Phantom and heard the harmony of a hundred voices singing in unison to a passionate *ranchera*. This fiesta was in full swing. Maybe right this moment wasn't the time to break the news about the whole mix-up. No one likes a party pooper.

Arturo escorted me up the stairs and said, "Welcome to *Casa del Flores!*"

Then he flung open the doors.

5

It was a fiesta, alright. In fact, if Jay Gatsby had thrown a party in the Mexican desert, it would've looked something like this. An extravaganza that most would never see. The opulence was absolute, from the patterned marble floors, vases of flowers perched in each corner, gold-framed oil paintings of rising suns and galloping stallions hanging on stucco walls, lit by bright chandeliers above.

Women in colored dresses filled the ballroom floor, surrounded by suited men with shiny shoes and slick hair, eyes fixed on the dancing beauties before them. There was laughter, shouts, and clinks of glasses. Parallel staircases curved upward like two snakes in a staring contest. Arturo said, "What do you think, *señor?*"

I made an attempt to play it smooth. "It's certainly a fine party."

A party which I had no business attending.

Across the dance floor, I counted a dozen older gentlemen in black *charro* jackets drinking at a bar. Each man had a sombrero, a mustache, and a shiny instrument resting beside him. *Portrait of a mariachi band on a break between sets.*

"Are you hungry, *señor?*" asked Arturo.

Come to think of it, I was. I hadn't eaten since I'd downed a dirt-cheap double cheeseburger back at LAX.

"Incredibly."

He led me through the revelers to an extensive buffet table.

"Consider it, as you like to say in America, an 'all-you-can-eat.' In the meantime, I will inform the boss of your arrival."

He bounded up the staircase, leaving me alone. Nothing stood between me and the greatest selection of food in all of Mexico: platters of steak, chorizo, and *al pastor* tacos, plates of golden *chilaquiles* with cheese and refried beans, and an abundance of different salsas; some red, some green, some marked *habanero*. For dessert, there was a fresh pot of creamy *arroz con leche* with apricot halves on top. But, right in front of me was the Mount Everest of quesadilla stacks, hot and steaming, the flour as white as the coastline sand. You could argue it would've looked suspicious *not* to dig in.

Sheepishly, I took one off the top, spooned on some habanero, and sank in my teeth. The heat of the beef, cheese, and salsa scalded my tongue, but I valiantly chewed on. I was three quesadillas deep, when a server appeared to replenish the stack.

"*Hola, señor,*" she said, doing a double-take. It was then I remembered my disheveled appearance. I would have been a sorry sight of a man no matter where I was, let alone at a scene of such glamour. The faded blue jeans. The flip flops. The three-day stubble. The tacky Hawaiian shirt, now stained with habanero—and the damned Fedora!

As I ate away my embarrassment, the mood of the party evolved. The guests cleared the dance floor. The music cut out. The twelve mariachis stood, picked up their instruments, and lifted their gaze to the balcony as if watching for a signal.

Then, a bride and groom stepped onto the interior balcony. So this was....*a wedding reception?* The crowd broke into applause as the newlywed couple smiled upon the fiesta. The groom was a handsome man in a gold-embroidered jacket and a matching sombrero; an impressive figure.

But, of course, the show belonged to the bride, whose jet-black hair fell over a white-lace dress stitched with green-stemmed roses. She had the smile of a pageant queen, but a pair of eyes that displayed no vanity; only an honest joy. The couple descended the staircase as the mariachis began to play a soft *canción*. When they reached the dance floor, the groom pulled the bride close and whispered something to her. Whatever he said made her smile grow wider, and I couldn't help but wonder what words he might have said.

The groom broke away from his bride and nodded to a mariachi, who passed him his guitar.

I had an idea of what was to follow. If, going by spaghetti westerns, it was to be an old-time serenade, a centuries-old tradition.

The groom began to play, plucking the strings with precision and care, circling his bride, their gaze never breaking. I felt an odd sense of privilege to be in the presence of such an iconic display, *especially* since I hadn't technically been invited.

The groom soon returned the guitar to the mariachi and took his bride by the hand. Holding her close, they began to step and twirl as one. A while later, an older couple joined, followed by another, and it wasn't long before the whole room danced together.

The bride couldn't have been more than twenty-five, but I guess she'd found her soul mate early. I wondered if I would ever dance with a bride who looked at me the way she looked at this noble groom. I erred on the side of doubt. For some of us, it was a conflicting sight. On one hand, you couldn't help but feel happy for the beautiful youngsters, but on the other, your heart soars with lonesome rage, envious that your own chance to catch that kind of flourishing young love is a long-sailed ship.

I was about to take another bite of the quesadilla when I saw a second woman in a crimson dress standing on the same balcony from which the newlyweds had emerged. She was probably in her early forties and bore an uncanny resemblance to the bride. Her face was a balance of beauty and strength. Her almond eyes and aquiline nose were features that told of her character; not a princess, but a power woman—more lioness, than damsel in distress. Her black hair reached the curve of her hips. The crimson dress looked so fine I nearly dropped the damn quesadilla.

And, lo and behold, she was staring right into my eyes. I suddenly heard no music. I saw no one else. Had time stopped just for us?

It seemed she was peering straight into my soul. I'd be damned if I could look away. Maybe I wanted her to see.

Finally, she nodded. But it wasn't just any nod. It was full of purpose and just between us.

Reciprocation was a must. I narrowed my gaze, flashed my best smile, and tipped the fedora, attempting the suave stroke of a chivalrous gentleman.

She held my gaze a second longer, then broke away. *Back to real-time, Galloway.*

The woman descended the stairs, turning every head in the room, eventually meeting the young bride in the center of the ballroom floor, where the two women embraced.

At first, you'd think they were sisters, but on closer look, there was a maternal gaze that could only be shared between a mother and daughter.

Christ, she must have had her young.

My thoughts were quickly interrupted by Arturo, who sprang from thin air. He put a hand on my shoulder and leaned in close. "The *jefe*," he said. "He's ready to meet."

I glanced back at the woman in the crimson dress, wishing I could watch just a little bit longer. *Goddammit, Arturo.*

"Right this second?"

"It's time, *señor*. Allow me to take your hat."

He beckoned a passing waiter, who hurried over.

Here was yet another chance to come clean. Removing the fedora would be a symbol of something, the final chance to speak the truth before I passed the point of no return.

Classic head and heart situation.

My head said to tell the truth. To admit the fedora wasn't mine. To say there had been a mistake! I was *not* the man they thought I was. Profuse apologies were in order, but surely they could understand that alcohol was to blame!

But my heart said to wait and find out more about the woman on the balcony, just until I had a chance to meet her in person, to behold the sight of her at point blank range. If I came clean now, I would never get that chance.

The waiter looked at Arturo.

Arturo looked at me.

I looked at the woman in red.

The twelve mariachis seemed to be looking at all of us.

I made my choice. With a confident smile, I removed the fedora and handed it to the waiter.

Everyone breathed a sigh of relief.

Time to meet the *jefe*.

6

Arturo led me up the staircase and down a shadowy hallway as the harmonious notes of mariachis fell away.

We passed a series of framed photos featuring a man
with dark bushy hair, thick eyebrows, and a clean-
shaven face.

In the first photo, he sat in a booth of a luxury
nightclub, encircled by suited gentlemen, their glasses
raised in a shared *salud*.

In the second photo, he stood with his arm around a
bare-chested, muscular boxer with a swollen right eye
and a championship belt around his waist.

The third photo was more recent. Beside the man
was the president of Mexico. Well, the *ex*-president—
he'd made headlines after being indicted on a long
history of corruption charges. It was said the start-up
funds for his political career had been linked back to
large donations of shady origins.

We came to a black wooden door at the end of the
hallway. Arturo knocked twice and eased it open. The
room was drowned in darkness, barely lit by the flames
of a corner fireplace.

Behind a wide, polished desk stood a frozen figure,
his face turned away, his hands clasped behind his
back. Arturo cleared his throat.

"Sir, I present to you, the one and only, *El Flamingo*."

Arturo backed away, and gently closed the door.

The man before me gazed through a panoramic window into the desert void, watching as if he waited long
enough, all life's answers would come to him in gentle whispers. He moved at last in a small but sudden
fashion, like a vampire waking from a thousand-year
sleep. When he turned around, our eyes met for the
first time.

It was the man from the photos in the hallway. He
was dressed in an expensive three-piece suit—black-

on-black-on-black. His hair was still bushy, but time had turned it silver to match a finely trimmed beard. The faint glimmer of the embers across the room revealed his darkest feature of all, his eyes, which held the slightest shine I could swear was a tear.

"So I finally see him in the flesh," he said. "*El Flamingo.*"

As he awaited a response, all I had to go on was my instincts. They told me to do the only thing I was ever any good at: acting. On that note, I took a long look at the man before me and nodded my head. "So they call me."

"Please forgive my emotions," he said.

He picked up a glass of what looked like mezcal, sipped, and closed his eyes. When he opened them, the tear had disappeared without ever falling.

"It's funny. In my life, I've seen many things. Ugly things. And I've never looked away. Yet, tonight, I couldn't stand to watch my daughter's wedding dance. The happiest day of her life, and here I was hiding away in an empty room. It really is strange, isn't it?"

"I'm sure it's been a big day," I said. "A mixed emotional response is to be expected."

He walked to me and offered his hand. There was no tight squeeze or who-can-crush-the-other-guy's-hand-the-most pissing match, but there was a cold rigidity in his grip.

"Diego Flores," he said. "*Mucho gusto.*"

Diego Flores.... Where the hell had I heard that name?

He gestured to his desk. "Take a seat, *compadre.*"

I sat down opposite and looked over his desk. The first thing I noticed was a small bottle lying on its side. There was no liquor inside, but a miniature pistol.

"Ah," said Diego. "*Una Pistola en una Botella.*"

A gun in a bottle. Like a ship in a bottle, but with a little more malice.

"It's a work of art, isn't it? Something that inspires me in many ways."

"Where did you find it?"

"*Estados Unidos,* of course, where guns are an art form. No one makes weapons quite like America."

"It's a nifty piece."

Beside the bottle was a brown leather notebook and a map of the Americas. Arrows, asterisks, and tiny indecipherable notes had been made on several points on the map: Argentina, Colombia, and all the way up to Toronto. On the left of the desk was a photograph that crushed me inside. It featured the woman in the crimson dress, the same one I'd just intimately locked eyes with. She had her arms wrapped around Diego's neck, and sadly for me, they looked head over heels in love. Diego caught me staring at the photograph.

"The love of my life. Nineteen years she's been beside me. *Hermosa, no?*"

Beautiful, no?

"Very," I said, aiming to keep it short. You never want to over-compliment a powerful man's wife.

Diego looked me up and down, from my knock-off *Havaianas* to my tacky, habanero-stained Hawaiian shirt. "Your chosen attire is interesting."

I felt my cheeks flush. I was about to apologize for the sheer lack of etiquette on my part, but Diego just smiled and shook his head like I was some kind of genius.

"But then again, they say you never see *El Flamingo* coming. A *gringo* idiot in a cheap Hawaiian shirt? Who would have guessed?"

I raised my hands in feigned humility. "The art of disguise, right?"

"Right. Did you receive the whiskey, *compadre?*"

"I did. *Muchas gracias, señor.*"

"How would you describe it?"

I made a show of thinking to myself. "Peaty. Very peaty."

"I figured you'd appreciate a little smoke. It was the least I could do for a man of your reputation. But for now, let's drink something a little more Mexican. Are you a big mezcal man?"

After the heavy consumption of cheap mezcal back at the tiki bar, the last thing I felt like was more of it, but it wasn't the time to be difficult. "The biggest," I answered.

He pulled out a decanter and a fresh glass from the drawer and poured me a double. I noticed there was another creature drowned by the substance, only this time it wasn't a worm. It was a scorpion.

"Neat?" asked Diego.

"There's no other way to drink mezcal."

Diego passed me the glass. I used the moment for a *beat,* as they say in acting, giving the mezcal a sniff, a swirl, and a patient sip.

"There are very few things left in this world that I trust," said Diego. "To me, trust is not a negotiation. Nor is it a puzzle with missing pieces. There can be no blemishes, no compromise. Your reputation is like stainless steel. Not easy to find today. Not in our line of work."

What line of work? Typesetting?

"Before tonight, I'd never seen your face. No one had. They talk of you as if you were a myth; a shadow. No one knows who you really are. Yet here I am, giving you my trust. It is why I wanted you for this job. It's not a job for a man. It's a job for a ghost. A job for *El Flamingo.*"

A knot formed in my stomach at the insertion of the word, "job," but I played along. "That's why I'm here."

"You must find the circumstances unusual," continued Diego. "A man of your profession brought into such an environment. A family environment. After all, I'm

just another client. Yet here you are. The legendary
El Flamingo, a guest at my daughter's wedding day.
Strange, no?"
"It's certainly not the norm. But you know how it is."
"How would you say it is?"
I tried to think of something broad to say that could
be applied to any field or industry. "Well. No two jobs
are the same."
He sharply turned his head. "Well, they certainly
end the same."
I gulped down half the mezcal. "That they do."
Diego stared into the flames of the fireplace, crackling over the music from below, which now seemed
worlds away.
"I'm sure a man of your craftsmanship will be in
search of the specifics. As they say, that is what sepa-
rates you from the others in your line of work. You're
a man with an appreciation of detail. But tonight, let's
cease the business talk. Love is in the air, and there is
a fiesta to enjoy. *Mañana puede esperar.*"
Tomorrow can wait.
We stood and shook hands once more when the door
burst open and the newlywed bride charged inside.
She halted about an inch from her father's face, shaking like a washing machine on spin cycle.
"*Mi único baile de bodas! ¿Y dónde está mi padre?
¡En su oficina, hablando de negocios con un pinche
gringo que nunca había visto antes!*"
My wedding dance and where is my father? In his
office, talking business with some fucking *gringo* I've
never seen before!
Arturo and the groom appeared in the doorway,
speechless and puffing, as the bride raged on. "*El día
de la boda de tu hija! ¡En su oficina!*"
Your daughter's wedding day! In your office!
"*¡Has estado en tu oficina toda mi vida!*"
You've been in your office my whole life!

Diego, Arturo, the groom, and I stood frozen, none of us saying a word; none of us having the stones to calm down the fuming young woman.

"*Y una vez más, mi padre está en silencio.*"

And one more time, my father is silent.

Before she stormed out, she met my eyes with a violent glare. For a second, I thought she might gouge out my eyes with her hot-pink fingernails.

"*And what kind of a fucking shirt is that?*"

"I sincerely apologize. I...uh...had planned for a beach wedding."

With a final scowl, she was gone, like a flash hailstorm. Arturo loosened his collar. The groom faced his new father-in-law. "*Lo siento, padre.*" Then to me. "My apologies, *señor.*"

"It's okay," I said. "She's right. It was a poor choice of shirt."

The groom nodded his respects and left the room. Arturo beckoned me to the door.

"Come, *señor*. Let's return to the party."

I thought I should acknowledge Diego, but his face was blank, his mind a thousand miles away. Maybe a daughter's rage can deafen one to hollow small talk. I followed Arturo out as Diego faced the desert void and turned to stone again.

7

I peered out from the same balcony where I'd first seen the newlyweds receive their welcome. The fiesta had died down significantly. The buffet had been removed and the barman had rolled-up his sleeves and was packing away bottles. A few last guests continued to dance, but lacked the same gusto they'd had in the younger night. I guess that's how weddings go when the bride storms out.

As for me, my head was all over the show. The peculiar sequence of events over the course of the evening had loosened my grasp on reality. If I were to refrain from losing my mind entirely, I would soon need to get some goddamn sleep. It was just that afternoon I'd arrived in Mexico, but so much had happened, it felt like days.

Between being mistaken for this *El Flamingo* character, then driven to a fiesta in the middle of the desert, meeting Diego, and finally, hearing about this obscure "job," well, it was a lot to take in.

There was no sign of the most beautiful woman in the world, but what was the point anyhow? She was a married woman; happily married for nineteen years to the filthy-rich, mansion-owning, whiskey-glass-inscribing Diego Flores. Which reminded me: where the hell had I heard that name?

Still far from sober, I wandered around in search of something to do or someone to talk to, but it seemed I was invisible to the remaining guests. The mariachis had boxed up their instruments and were heading out.

"*La música fue muy bien,*" I said as they passed.

They ignored me as they loaded their instruments into a red travel bus. A wild thought struck me: Why not just blend in with this group of exhausted musicians? Flee the scene as the thirteenth mariachi. It would be the perfect camouflage. All I needed was an extra sombrero and I would have my escape. No one knew my name, where I was from, or where I was headed. I'd be an untraceable man in a country far too large to ever track down. It all would have worked, if only there was another sombrero in sight. Which there wasn't. Sometimes, even in Mexico, an extra sombrero is too much to ask.

Arturo appeared and gave each of the mariachis a handshake and a white envelope. Probably cash. He seemed to be many things: chauffeur, butler, and a constant pair of eyes and ears. I wondered if he ever caught a moment's rest. The mariachis hopped into the van and drove off into the desert, taking with them my last chance to abscond.

Exhaustion began to take hold of me. If I could find a place to sleep, maybe I'd wake to find I'd dreamed the whole shebang. I wandered from the foyer through a curving corridor into a spacious kitchen. Everything was sparkling silver, except for a few stacks of plates atop the center island. A trio of housekeepers was washing and drying dishes. I was about to offer to give them a hand when I heard a voice behind me. Arturo, springing from nowhere, once again.

"*Señor*, there you are. You must be tired. Allow me to escort you to your quarters."

Quarters. Nice.

We climbed the stairs again, this time to level three. A few weaves and turns later, we arrived at a door at the end of the hallway.

"Our corner suite, *señor*. The finest room, reserved only for our most esteemed guests. The late, great Juan Gabriel was the last gentleman to enjoy this room."

"Incredible."

The door clicked open to reveal a space that could fit my old apartment three times over. It had turquoise walls and a floor-to-ceiling window that overlooked a lagoon pool where tiki torches cast shadows over the courtyard. In the distance, the taillights of departing cars faded into the night.

The king-sized bed was made up with silk sheets. Soft, inviting, and wide enough to sleep sideways, I didn't care which way I slept, so long as I just got to shut my damn eyes.

There were two doors in the room. One led to a double wardrobe and the other to the bathroom, where there was both a walk-in shower and a huge oval bathtub. I'm sure Juan Gabriel had been thoroughly impressed, whoever the hell he was.

Arturo motioned to a telephone on the bedside table. "If you need anything else, *señor*, do not hesitate to call. Just dial star."

With that, he left me alone. I kicked off my shoes and collapsed onto the bed.

A short time later, however, I awoke to some kind of stirring. I sat up and wiped the drool from my mouth. It must've come from the hallway. Footsteps?

Under the doorframe, the light went dark.

Someone was right outside.

An assailant? An armed man sent to kill the imposter who allowed himself to adopt the title of the famed *"El Flamingo?"* Maybe it was Diego himself. Maybe that damned desert had whispered the truth to him after all.

I eased out of bed and crept toward the door. A bullet could shoot through any second, and I'd be dead before hearing the blast.

Instead, I heard something else.

Three small, stealthy knocks.

Carefully, I opened the door.

To my amazement, it was *her*—the woman from the balcony. The mother of the bride. The wife of Diego Flores. What in God's name was she doing here? Seeing her from a distance had taken my breath away, but up close, she just about stopped my heart. She wore a silk robe tied in a knot around her waist, and the moonlight glow made her resemble a hologram that would flicker away and be lost forever if I dared reach out and touch her.

But her eyes carried a message of some kind. A warning.

She looked down the hallway, put a finger to her lips, and gave the slightest shake of her head.

Don't talk.

Then, she leaned into me.

Time slowed down.

The concept of gravity ceased to exist.

Was she going in for the kiss?

Her perfume smelled like vanilla, roses, and some other secret ingredient. Light-headed, I closed my eyes, ready to feel her lips on mine. This was happening, and there was nothing I could do but accept it. To take it like a man!

But instead, she leaned right past me as her hair brushed my neck and gave me goosebumps. Gently, she passed me a small wooden object of some kind.

"This is it," she whispered. "Guard it with your life."

Then she slipped away, back down the hallway and into the darkness, like a mermaid into an ocean void.

I stood there, reeling from her touch, both extraordinarily aroused and incredibly confused.

I inspected the object in my hand—a wooden cross on a strand of redwood rosary beads. I'd never been a man of God, but I'd seen these before, usually dangling from the rearview mirror of passing cars in L.A. traffic.

What could this mean? That she wanted me to find God? To accept Jesus as my savior? To join her passing out bible tracts in Tijuana? Doubtful. There had to be more to it.

I paced the room, trying to piece things together.

Deep breaths, Lou. Deep breaths.

This woman was an enigma, and her secret visit to my quarters had only widened the scope of mystery. What was *it?* Why did *it* need guarding with my life? If only she'd appeared in my quarters simply to push me onto the enormous bed to have her way with me. What a welcome to Mexico that would have been. I wanted complete blackness to block out all confusion. The curtains, of course, were electronic, controlled by a small device. With the click of a button, they moved together until the room became completely dark. It was at that moment I remembered where I'd heard the name *Diego Flores.*

About a year before, I'd auditioned for a bit-part in a TV series, a biopic dramatization of a crime lord's rise, a violent ascent that left him with the number one spot on the F.B.I.'s Most Wanted List. The show was named after his infamous pseudonym.

El Buitre.

The Vulture.

El Buitre's real name was Diego Flores. The same Diego Flores who had just become my new boss, whose wife just paid me a secret visit in the midnight hour. Oh, what a tangled web I'd woven.

I thought back to everything I'd heard over the last few hours. *El Flamingo*'s reputation. A dangerous world. My clients. No one had ever laid eyes on *El Flamingo* until now. When I'd borrowed his fedora, I'd assumed his identity.

All jobs end the same, Diego had said.

I was beginning to suspect *El Flamingo*'s chosen profession was that of a contract killer. Or, as they say in *Español*, a *sicario.*

Typesetting, huh?

I just knew it was bullshit.

8

The last time I'd seen my father was twenty-four years before I ever set foot in Mexico. He was on a hospital bed behind a dull curtain, his skin ghost-white, his eyes perpetually closed. I suspected I was dreaming, stuck in the recollection of a twenty-four-year-old memory, but I could have been fooled.

I'd been sitting in a seventh-grade science lesson, trying to piece together an attempt at a hypothesis for some chemical experiment, when a man in a charcoal suit entered the class and asked to speak to my teacher, Ms. McLean. He was short, heavy, and utterly impassive. I watched them talk through the square window of the classroom door, and I could sense bad news would follow. This was because Ms. McLean had put her hand to the side of her face, and you knew when she did that, it was never a good sign.

Maybe you'd failed the end-of-term test, or it was your turn to see the school nurse for a dreaded injection. Not that day. That day, it was something worse.

Ms. McLean reentered the room while the man in the suit waited outside. She crouched down next to me, looked me in the eye, and spoke in a tone so soft I struggled to hear.

"Lou. You're excused for the day, love."

"Why am I excused?"

"You need to go with that man. He's your family lawyer."

I didn't know much about lawyers, and I didn't care much for meeting one.

"But I just started my hypothesis."

A twelve-year-old Lou Galloway fights the inevitable.

I knew what was coming. It was gonna be about my dad. My mum had told me he'd been fighting a flu; that he was "under the weather." But that was last spring, and now it was halfway through fall. No one had the flu for that long. I might've sucked at science, but I wasn't an idiot.

I remember turning back to look through the class-room door, wishing I could've just stayed in there and finished the damn hypothesis. As boring as it was, it was better than whatever the hell would follow.

The man in the suit led us down a bleak corridor, hurried and business-like. "Your father's not coming back, son," he said. "He's not coming back."

9

I woke to the buzz of the parting electronic curtains as a beam of sunlight expanded across my face. I felt like a dead body dug up from the big sleep, with no idea of what, where, or who I was.

"*Buenos dias, señor.*"

Arturo stood at my bedside, hovering over me like he'd been there for hours. He wore a pressed maroon suit, and in his hand was a cup of coffee. It was all coming back to me now.

"Asking forgiveness, *señor?*" he asked.

I cleared my throat. "Excuse me?"

Arturo pointed to the rosary beads in my hand. I must've fallen asleep clutching them.

"The cross, *señor.* Praying away your past sins?"

I sat up and tried to look earnest, like a true man of God.

"And all the ones to come," I said. "Nothing helps like a chat with Jesus."

"*Si, señor.* That, and a little *café.*"

Arturo passed me the cup, steam dancing from its wide rim. The day instantly seemed a little more faceable. Anyone who brings you a strong brew first thing in the morning is worth your trust.

"*Café negro, señor. Fuerte.*"

Strong black coffee.

I took a sip, and it hit me fast, blasting the sleep dust out of my eyes. From the proud look on his face, I'd say he'd brewed it himself.

"What's the time?" I asked.

"Just before ten, *señor.* Breakfast will be served in the dining room in thirty minutes, where you will be joined by *Señor Flores* and his wife, Maria-Carla."

Maria-Carla. Her name had a sweet ring to it. The thought of seeing her again jousted my heart rate. A shower was in order.

40

"What's the attire?"

"Ahh. You'll find a selection of clothing in the wardrobe. The choice is yours, *señor.*"

"*Gracias*, Arturo. I'll see you down there."

I downed the rest of the coffee, hopped out of bed, and admired the morning view of the courtyard below. The garden flowers surrounding the lagoon pool resembled a tropical paradise, smack-bang in the middle of a desert. Maybe it was a mirage?

After a quick shower, I inspected my wardrobe selection. I picked out a navy-pinstripe polo and a pair of white slacks, the kind of outfit the crème-de-la-crème of hired-guns might wear. As for the rosary beads, I'd rolled them up and tucked them into my shoe.

On my way to breakfast, I stopped at the same balcony that overlooked the ballroom. There was no trace of the guests who'd filled the place the night before. What had been a place of festive glamour now seemed more like an abandoned ghostly kingdom.

I followed the aroma of grilling spices toward the dining room. I was hungry enough to eat a horse, but chose to focus on the thought of an authentic Mexican breakfast, not the thought of Diego's searching eyes looking for slip-ups or signs that something may be off. All I had to do was avoid saying anything that wouldn't come from the lips of a world-class assassin. Easy enough?

It's the actor's job to overcome performance nerves. They must not try to impress. They have to be present, submerged in a deep state of focus and relaxation. Only then can authenticity be grasped. With this in mind, I entered the dining room.

Diego Flores sat at the head of the polished oak dining table, sipping from a small espresso cup. He wore a blood-red shirt, his hair was freshly combed, and the morning light exposed the Botox-stiffened skin of his face. A large oil painting hung on the wall behind him, depicting a game of cards between two men in a dim room. Their faces were lit only by a fire, the smoke of which formed the shape of a Devil's shadow watching over the hand at play.

"Here is our guest," Diego said.

At the opposite end of the table sat Maria-Carla, wearing a lime green blouse with the top two buttons undone. She gave me a smile that was nothing like the warning look in her eyes just a few hours before.

"I don't believe you had the chance to meet my wife last night," said Diego.

My mouth went dry, but Maria-Carla answered for both of us.

"No. We didn't. But I did notice you enjoying the quesadillas," she teased.

"He is a new business associate of mine," said Diego. "Someone I've wanted to work with for a long time. He handles certain contract work."

Contract work. Classic.

"They call him *El Flamingo*. Have a seat."

I took a chair in the middle of the table. Diego on my right, Maria-Carla on my left. Maria-Carla raised her eyebrows. "Does this mean I call you *Señor* Flamingo?"

"I don't insist on formality," I said. "Just *Flamingo* is fine by me."

"It's an interesting title."

"An expression of my individuality," I said. No choice but to own it.

"That can't be your real last name."

"It's his pseudonym," said Diego.

"And what kind of contract work do you do?" she asked.

Only one thing came to mind. "Typesetting."

"Typesetting?"

"The sales end."

The spices continued to sizzle, as Maria-Carla considered my response. "And how would you describe typesetting?"

I gulped, desperately trying to remember how the hell the stranger had described it. "It's the composition of text by arranging physical types or their digital equivalents," I managed. "You know, this is a beautiful dining room."

"It sounds very administrative."

"Extremely so. Numbers. Charting graphs. Decimal points. Tedious details. To expand would be to subject you to colossal boredom." I swigged down some more coffee. "And again, this really is a *lovely* dining room."

Determined to move the conversation along, I asked after the newlyweds.

"They left for their honeymoon this morning," said Maria-Carla.

"Where did they go?"

"The islands," said Diego.

"The islands? Very nice. Barbados? Jamaica?"

"Around there."

In the kitchen, a rotund chef stirred the contents of a frying pan. Diego said her name was Consuela, and that she had a Michelin star to her name. He said he had poached her away from the finest restaurant in Guadalajara to cook exclusively for him.

"As you know, *señor*, I hire only the best."

"So why do they call you *El Flamingo*?" asked Maria-Carla, sipping orange juice from a champagne flute.

Diego cut in. "I believe for his choice of colorful shirts. Isn't that right, *señor*?"

I nodded along. "Again, a continued expression of my individuality."

"And why do you choose to wear flamboyant shirts?" pressed Maria-Carla.

It was a test. A ping-pong game of subtext, forcing me to improvise my way out of a tightening corner.

"As you know, I work in typesetting."

"So you mentioned."

"Typesetting can be...dense work."

I employed a dramatic pause, fighting to make up an answer. "I wear flamboyant shirts because, well, in my line of work, one can always use a little color."

Maria-Carla tilted her head, unconvinced at the weak explanation, but Diego offered a satisfied nod. "There you have it."

Leave them wanting more, Lou. Now, change the damn subject.

"So, where did you two meet?"

Maria-Carla peered out the dining room window where the horizon pointed south to worlds beyond.

"Colombia," she said.

"Colombia?"

Diego smiled reminiscently, his mind traveling back to another time and place.

"I was there on business, and some associates took me out to a local cantina that looks across the valley. I was admiring the view when I heard a voice begin to sing. It was an old Mexican song about a woman with no friend left in the world except the withering cigarette in her hand. When I turned, I'd never seen a pair of eyes like the ones that looked back at me. From the second I saw her, I had to have her. I knew she would be mine."

It sounded a little creepy, but I didn't say so. You gotta read the room.

"Those same eyes stare at me now. I fell in love that night, and I've been trapped ever since."

Maria-Carla did not blink as she eyed her husband.

"But that's a long story," said Diego. "And today is a short day."

Consuela dished three small portions into separate bowls and brought them to the table.

"Huevos Rancheros."

"Wait 'til you taste the spice," said Diego.

The poached eggs simmered in the rich tomato sauce while the scent of herbs and melted cheese came enticingly through the air. As soon as we dug in, I could almost taste the Michelin star.

"After breakfast, let's take a walk in the gardens," he said.

Maria-Carla lowered her voice in a mock whisper. "That means he wants to talk business."

Diego devoured the last of his meal with a passion. It seemed to be more than just breakfast to him, a reminder of something, perhaps. They say the best meals take you back to a place in time you wish to be again. I wondered what that place was for a man like Diego. He put his knife and fork together and watched me.

"Can you taste the spices, *compadre*?"

"I can."

"It's not too hot?"

"It's hot," I said, my mouth seriously on fire, "but I'm handling it."

Then he sharpened his gaze and edged forward, allowing me to see why they called him, *The Vulture*.

"Good," he said. "It's important you experience the heat."

10

Diego's backyard had the character of a carefully cultivated botanical garden. Fresh-trimmed grass bordered the walkways that twirled through the colorful maze. Assortments of roses and other varieties of floral exotica gave off a crisp scent, a contrast to the dry death of the encompassing desert.

"The flowers bring me great peace," said Diego. "It's like you said at breakfast. In our line of work, one needs a little color."

The mansion was well behind us. Diego put his hands in his pockets and dropped his tone. "There are many by-products of our business, aren't there?"

"Too many to count."

"One of them is violence. It is quite simply inevitable."

He said it like a trucker would tell you that at some point along the road, you're gonna have to stop for gas.

"I have good news, and I have bad news."

"Let's start with the bad," I answered.

Diego paused, inhaling the mountain breeze. "We're about to go to war."

A chill went down my spine, but I tried to look casual like we were shooting the shit over the daily mundanities of life; like the weather, the economy, last night's ball game.

"War," I repeated. "With who?"

"A Colombian. His name is Juan Moreno. He is a politician in the city of Cali who is beginning to cause me problems."

I'd learned from watching countless thrillers that there are two sure phrases to use when you don't know what the hell is going on, but have to appear like a man of intellectual competence: *"I'm not sure I follow,"* or the more straightforward, *"Go on."* I decided to see-saw between the two, using whichever was more appropriate.

"I'm not sure I follow."

"You could say he has a...strong moral code."

I drew up a studied gaze. "Go on."

"This moral code of his has become an annoyance. He has taken a certain stance that has become detrimental to the progression of my business. A stone in my way, you could say."

"What did he do?"

"It's more about what he won't do. He is an idealistic man. A man invested in the concepts of change. You see, he holds a large degree of influence. The people see him as a hero. During the elections, he was quite the public speaker. He sold his people on a dream I think even he believes."

"What's that?"

"That good will prevail."

We arrived at a small clubhouse a little way from the mansion, maybe half a mile or so. There was a polished-wood bar stocked with fine liquors, a wide poker table, and the faint smell of cigar smoke from nights gone by. We passed through a side door and out onto a row of sheltered wooden units that watched over the desert horizon.

A driving range.

"I come here to find clarity," said Diego.

The landscape resembled a backdrop for an old-time western. In the distance was a mountain range, desolate and uncharted. The mountains were steep, jagged creations, like massive blades cutting into the clouds. If they could speak, they'd tell you not to go in there, to turn around and go back the way you came.

"How about we have a few swings?"

Diego took up a bucket of golf balls and a silver driver from a rack on the wall. He chose a unit halfway down and lined up a shot. After a couple of practice swings, he brought the club down with a crack. The ball disappeared into the sky, and we never saw it hit the ground.

"A long time ago, I was sent to Colombia," said Diego. "The purpose was to develop certain business partnerships. I was young and hungry to prove myself, so I volunteered. At that time, I was working with a much more flexible businessman. Not such an idealist. More of a realist. He ensured our product was able to be transported with fluidity. Competition was kept to a minimum. Law enforcement was made happy. Profits were impressive."

Diego teed up another ball and fired away. Another toy for the prairie dogs.

"Since Moreno has entered the equation, things haven't continued as I would have hoped. He introduced an initiative that I will admit has had greater effect than I first predicted. He calls it *La hoja de ruta para salir de la corrupción.*"

The roadmap out of corruption.

A lump formed in my throat. The stakes were getting too damn high. This was no game for a failed actor. I thought of making a break for it, dashing into the wild winds of the desert. I liked my chances with the snakes and sandstorms a whole lot better than whatever the hell might follow.

"I've never liked the word *corruption*," he said. "It warps one's ability for reasonable conversation."

I said what I thought he would want to hear. "Yes. I imagine such a word would be inappropriate for use at the business table."

"Moreno has exposed certain colleagues of mine who were paramount to my business operations. He has outed political, military, and law enforcement personnel who were key players on my team. This has resulted in a significant loss in profit. It has gone far enough. I have tried to dissuade him from his ideals. I have made him offers that are more than generous, all to no avail."

"So, what happens now?"

"A game of cards," said Diego.

"Cards?"

"Poker. He is an avid player. As am I. Do you play?" *Stay calm, Galloway. Answer the question.* "Sure. I've been to Vegas."

"And what is the golden rule?"

I took a stab in the dark. "Know when to hold 'em. Know when to fold 'em."

Diego gave a satisfied nod. "Exactly, *compadre*. In this sense, Moreno has made a mistake. He has failed to identify his best interests. His position has remained inflexible. It seems he values his moral code more than any kind of financial gain. I don't trust men who can't be bought. They are unpredictable."

Diego stared out to the desert. "Moreno is, at heart, a Don Quixote. A fool. A dreamer. And dreamers never win. Not in this world."

A Don Quixote? The more I heard about this Juan Moreno, the more I respected him.

Diego handed me the driver. My turn. I hoped he wouldn't notice the tremble in my hands. Composure was everything. I placed the ball on the tee and stared toward the mountains, picturing the stillness of the man who sold typesetting.

What would *El Flamingo* do? By God, he would keep his poise. I kept my eye on the ball, drew the club back, then let it fly. *Thwack.* Like a gunshot. The ball disappeared far into the horizon. It might have even flown farther than Diego's.

"*Muy bien,*" said Diego.

"*Gracias.*"

"Three days from now, Juan Moreno and I will sit down for a game of poker. He has granted me one last opportunity to discuss our prospective futures."

Diego removed a cigar from his shirt pocket and lit up with the flick of a steel Zippo. Carved into the metal was the silhouette of a woman clutching a microphone.

"However, the situation is not as it appears."

"How so?"

"If there was a deal at hand, it would've been done by now. I believe he is keeping me close in order to expose my business interests. I have no choice but to make a pre-emptive strike. That's where you come in."

Diego leaned forward and intertwined his fingers.

"*El Flamingo*, you are going to kill Juan Moreno."

11

"But first, you are to accompany my wife on a trip."

Another curveball, just while I was trying not to break out in a panic attack. "Excuse me, sir?"

"You are to travel to Colombia alongside Maria-Carla forty-eight hours before I arrive. I have arranged accommodation at a hotel there, *La Vela de Cali*. I am the majority owner. It is the safest location available."

I loved the idea of an all-expenses-paid vacation away with his uncomfortably beautiful wife, but I couldn't see the logic in involving her. I put on a professional, concerned tone.

"If you don't mind me asking, *señor*, why put her in harm's way?"

Diego looked to the floor and offered a sad shrug. "Because I no longer trust her."

Easy, Lou. Tread carefully. "What makes you say that?"

"I suspect my circle may have a leak. As much as it breaks my heart to say, I believe it to be her."

Which might explain her visit to my quarters the night before. "I see. I'm sorry."

"Don't be. Everyone betrays eventually."

We let the silence brew, almost to the point of discomfort.

"She will believe I am sending you with her as protection. This is not untrue, but I need you to be close to her, to watch her every move."

"I'll be right by her side."

"The two of you will not be *totally* alone. You will be accompanied by Arturo, who assists me in all my operations. Tomorrow morning, you will be flown to Colombia."

"Who are we flying with?"

Diego shot me a stern look. "I have my own jet, Flamingo."

Of course he did. "Of course you do."

"I will arrive two days later. We will meet Juan Moreno at a private club to play our game of cards. You will be introduced as a valued business associate of mine. You will have a seat at the table. When the time is right, you will strike. Preferably after I win. I would like to see him lose one more time before he dies."

I took a deep breath, the panic attack still bubbling beneath the surface. "Seems pretty straightforward."

"Moreno will, of course, have a security detail. You will be searched before you enter. Therefore, you will be unarmed. But it is said that you are just as lethal without a gun as you are with one."

What the hell could I say? "I'm not one to lie on my résumé."

"Forgive my curiosity, but I heard you once eliminated an entire chapter of bikers with nothing but a pencil?"

"A *sharp* pencil," I confirmed.

"And you once blew up an 18th Street gang with nothing but a pack of Tic-Tacs and a can of Pepsi?"

I smiled as if lost in a fond memory. "All eighteen of 'em."

He peered at me, astonished, and shook his head. "My whole life, I've been able to read people. Except you, *Flamingo*. When I look at you, I see nothing."

Just like those bastard producers back in L.A. "It's my job to be unreadable."

"Everyone knows your name, but not your face. You are a master of disguise, it seems. An actor extraordinaire."

Words I'd been wanting to hear my whole life. "*Gracias*," I said. "It came at a cost."

"Which was?"

"Time, mainly."

Diego's smile fell away. He stepped toward the horizon and crossed his hands behind his back.

"Ahh, time. Yes. Time is money they always say. But they're wrong. Money comes and goes. You make some, you lose some, you make it back again. But time—"

He paused. "Time will always be running out."

Later that night, I returned to my quarters in a state of dread.

I'd managed to charge my phone back to life for the first time in twenty-four hours. It was back on no more than ten minutes when it started to buzz. My agent, Tommy—again.

I spoke in a hushed whisper.

"Tommy. You can't keep calling me."

"You kidding me? Most actors spend their whole life waiting for their agent to call. You ungrateful prick!"

I'd expected this kind of outrage. "Tommy, I can't hear what you're saying. The reception is trash. I'm in a desert."

"Yeah? I'm in a desert, too. You might've heard of it. It's called L.A. You know that place where you came to become a fuckin' star? Listen. You gotta get back here. Pronto. I got an opportunity coming through. Something big, kid. Something huge."

Tommy had been saying he had *something big* coming through for as long as I'd known him. You had to take it with a grain of salt.

"I can't right now, Tommy."

"The reception is bad, Galloway. It sounded like you said you *can't*."

"I'm not coming back to L.A.!"

"Jesus Christ. You fell in love, didn't you? It's a goddamn woman isn't it."

"Oh, man."

"It's a man?"

"No, it's not a man."

"It's fine if it *is* a man!"

"I know that Tommy! It's not the point!"

"You fell in love down there with some gorgeous guy or gal and now you've forgotten who the hell you are. But I'll tell you right now. You're an actor, Galloway. The only person you should be falling in love with is yourself!"

I thought about Maria-Carla. Her entrancing gaze. The midnight visit. The incredible perfume. Maybe Tommy was right—I gave him a sub-par confession.

"Fine, Tommy. You want the truth? It's about a woman. And it's not safe to talk right now. I gotta go. *Adios.*"

"But you're not listening, I got you a—"

I hung up before he could finish his sentence.

The time was just after midnight, which meant that, in less than five hours, Maria-Carla and I would be flown in Diego's private jet to Colombia, a far-away land I'd only read about in books and seen in films.

Part of me was watching myself from the outside, a character in my own story, with no real sense of what would happen next. Perhaps I was existing in a fictional world. Maybe none of it was real. But, stop; thinking like that can drive a man *loco.*

I decided to take a bath, clear my head, and figure out how to navigate this pickle.

If I was going to survive, I'd have to take everything as it came; day by day, moment to moment. The thing was, I had a responsibility that couldn't be ignored. This was no longer just about me. The fate of another human being had found its way into my hands. Juan Moreno was a good man, fighting the good fight for the sake of his people. He knew nothing of Lou Galloway, a hapless stranger who'd been tasked with taking his life.

I stepped out of the bath, dried off, and checked myself in the mirror. Rugged stubble had made its mark on my once boyish face. Under my eyes were lines from sleepless nights and California sun. I still had most of my sandy blonde hair, though it was starting to gray, and I still got called handsome every now and again. I supposed I could pass for the real *El Flamingo*. He had the look of a guy that was perpetually in his forties, and sure as shit, I was getting there too. But a similarity in appearance is only one thing. What matters most is what lies behind the eyes.

The legend of *El Flamingo*—his reputation, his deeds, his gravitas…. Could I really pull that off?

The anxiety of earlier was on its way back. I forced myself to take long, slow inhalations. In through the nose, out through the mouth. I put a hand on my heart, willing it to slow down.

Then a remarkable thing happened. A calm washed over me, the way it used to when I was an actor just about to step on stage. Instead of panicking, I made a choice: to be wholeheartedly unafraid.

Standing there like a lunatic in nothing but a bath towel, I closed my eyes. My pulse slowed. My breaths lightened. My hands ceased to tremble. It was like a message to a Jedi Warrior from *The Force*. Maybe this was the start of something beautiful. In all those years spent chasing a dream, I'd never been part of a cause greater than myself.

Diego Flores represented a certain kind of evil. He was a profiteer and a murderer—corruption personified. Guys like him made the world the cesspool it was, but here was a chance, in my own absurdly unconventional way, to fight for something that mattered. I hadn't studied martial arts. I didn't know how to shoot a gun. I'd never come under fire. Yet I was strangely qualified for the task at hand.

I was an *actor*. *El Flamingo* was my *character*.

It was as simple as that.

I wouldn't run. I had trained my whole life for this. No longer would I be the worm, drowned at the bottom of a mezcal bottle. I was destined to be the *mariposa*. I would play the role of *El Flamingo*.

I found a freshly steamed, dark navy, three-piece suit and a pink shirt hanging in the wardrobe. On the table was a note, signed by Arturo: *Clothes and accessories for the next three days, señor. I hope the suit fits.*

It did. Staring into the mirror, I saw the suit was instantly transformative. Returning my gaze was not Lou Galloway, the failed actor, but *El Flamingo*, the assassin. A man who can blend in anywhere; move like a shadow. A man trained to survive; to kill. A man who remains cool, calm, and collected in the face of chaos.

As an actor, the first step to playing the character is believing you *are* the character. If you don't believe, then no one else will.

I peered at the man in the mirror. "Hello."

He didn't look away, and neither did I.

"They call you *El Flamingo*. I need you to take the wheel for a while."

There was no fear in his eyes as the shadows of the room enclosed us. In that moment, we reached an understanding. For the next three days, I would use every skill I'd ever learned throughout my unseen acting career. To survive, I would have to portray the most lethal assassin in the world. But when the time came, I would seize control of the narrative. I was *not* going to kill Juan Moreno.

I was going to save his life.

12

In the dark of a looming dawn, Maria-Carla and I were driven to an airstrip about a mile from the mansion, where Diego's private jet waited. It was dark silver, with broad wings and a sharp nose like a sniffing vulture.

Diego accompanied us on the drive. He wore a dressing gown, as if he'd just gotten out of bed, but his eyes were those of an unrested man. He pulled Maria-Carla close, brushed her hair to the side, and whispered something in her ear. After escorting her up the jet-stairs, he returned to the ground, where we shared a parting exchange.

"Remember, Flamingo. Her every move."

"I'll be watching."

He studied me a moment longer, then said, "You're a handsome man, Flamingo. I have no doubt it is something you have been told before."

"Not often," I answered.

"I'm sure it is an observation that has passed through the mind of my wife."

Receiving his warning loud and clear, I told him there was nothing to worry about. That I was a consummate professional.

"Until Colombia, Flamingo."

"Until Colombia."

Inside, the jet looked more like a cocktail lounge than the interior of an aircraft. Crisp white walls. Tan seats. A minibar in the rear corner. I chose a reclining massage chair toward the back, which made for one hell of a window seat.

Al Pacino was at the front of the plane, his face filling the frame of a large, flat-screen television. *Godfather, Part Two*. Spanish subtitles. It was the scene where a young Michael Corleone stares down his weaker brother with cold, dark eyes.

"You're nothing to me anymore," he told him.

Maria-Carla sat opposite me. She wore fitted blue jeans and a black leather jacket, and her hair was tied back in a ponytail. No longer did she appear like a rich man's trophy wife, but a woman on a mission who could be stopped by nothing. I noticed she paid close attention to the scene between the Corleone brothers.

Arturo slid out of the cockpit door. "Soon, we will take off. Is there anything I can offer?"

Add flight attendant to his ever-growing résumé.

"*¿Puedes girar la televisión, por favor?*" asked Maria-Carla.

Can you turn off the television, please?

"*Por supuesto, señora.*"

The screen went black, and Corleone was gone. Maybe she had seen enough of angry men with cold eyes. Arturo took the seat closest to the cockpit door, allowing him to watch over the entire cabin.

The engines fired up and a swarm of butterflies set off in my stomach. We circled around and proceeded down the runway. The jet accelerated. Maria-Carla looked over her shoulder. Our eyes met, but I offered only a brief smile. Un-flirtatious. Professional. I looked back out the window but could feel her eyes remain on me. I wondered what her instincts were telling her.

She tapped her knuckles against the armrest. Maybe she was a nervous flyer like I was.

I mean, like *Lou* was.

Nothing, however, could rattle the nerves of *El Flamingo*, and, as of that early morning, we were one and the same.

We became airborne, then headed skyward and south as the seal of darkness was broken by a blue and orange horizon. Behind us, the mansion lights faded to nothing as we soared over the jagged mountain range. It's funny how perceptions change. Yesterday the mountains had resembled sharp blades stabbing the clouds, but today they were arrows, urging us onward. Aside from the occasional farmhouse below, all to be seen was the vast expanse of the dry red desert.

A short time later, Arturo fell asleep, his head cocked back, a loud snore coming from the gorse of his mustache.

Maria-Carla slipped out of her seat and headed for the rear bathroom. As she passed me, she made the slightest tilt of her head. Was it just me, or did she want me to follow her in? Could this be another of her secret *sotto voce* exchanges?

If I was wrong, I would look like the creepiest bastard in the universe. But I remembered what she'd told me in the doorway of my room a couple of nights ago.

This is it. Guard it with your life.

I had to figure *it* out and preferably before we got to Colombia.

What the hell.

I gave it a few seconds, then followed suit. I knocked three times on the bathroom door, just the way she had the other night.

The door slid open.

Maria-Carla grabbed my shirt, yanked me inside, and swiftly locked the door.

I held my breath as she inspected my person. The same rose and vanilla perfume made my head spin. Her full breasts were pushed up against my chest. My heart was a beat away from popping out of my suit jacket. Our eyes were locked, and our lips were well within kissing distance.

"You read my mind," she said.

What would *El Flamingo* do? Surely, he would keep his poise in the face of a quintessential femme-fatale. Wouldn't he?

"A simple deduction," I offered.

"Listen," she said. "I suspect we have a leak."

The *exact* same thing Diego said.

"How can you be sure?" I asked.

"I have an inkling."

Her voice was low, breathy, and impossible to resist. I matched her tone. "Then we have to assume the worst."

"In which case, there is a possibility he knows."

Who knows? And *what* did he know?

I gazed into her eyes, attempting to look like a man who knew what the hell was going on. "A possibility... that he *knows*?" I queried.

"Who I really am," she finished.

That was key. I wasn't the only one with something to conceal. I needed to buy some time.

"This leak," I said. "It could be anyone."

"Exactly. It could be on my side. It could be on theirs. It could even be you."

"Or you," I shot back.

"Touché."

"Touché, Wednesday, Thursday," I winked.

"What?"

"Nothing. The point is, why send me away with you two days before he arrives in Colombia?"

"Because he suspects you too."

I was flirting with danger, needing to say just enough to appear in the know, but not so much as to give myself away. *Think like El Flamingo.*

"It certainly was peculiar timing."

"If we have been compromised, then all we have is what I gave you. Is it safe?"

The beads were still in my shoe, and they were becoming highly irritating. "It's safe."

She looked me over one more time, then said, "You're not what I thought you'd be, Flamingo."

"That's what they all say."

"You know we can't trust anyone."

"Not even each other?"

"Not even each other. But..."

"But?"

"I've got a feeling we have to."

A strangely comfortable silence followed, a moment of intimacy between two relative strangers, 40,000 feet in the air.

"I'll be watching your back, Flamingo."

Maria-Carla twisted the handle and slipped out.

"And I yours—"

She shut the door in my face before I could finish my sentence. Highly embarrassed, I took a moment to recompose, then used the facilities. All this talk of leaks had left me in need of one myself. When I returned to my seat, Arturo was still snoring like a rhino with an awful flu. How he hadn't woken himself was truly astonishing.

I stared out the window and considered the puzzle at hand. Who the hell was the leak? What information had escaped? That Diego was planning a hit on Juan Moreno? Could word of the mythical *El Flamingo*'s involvement have slipped out? That he was the cornerstone of the assassination plot? Did someone suspect I was an impostor? And, as for the real *El Flamingo*, where in the world had he gone?

But, most of all, who was Maria-Carla? What was she withholding from her husband? Or, could this be an elaborate double-bluff, the ever-loyal spouse playing disloyal to expose the traitor within? I'd seen all the Bond films. I knew the femme fatale's power. Sensuality is a torture method used to extract information from even the most resistant of warriors. Nothing clouds a straight man's mind like a woman's allure.

Then again, maybe Maria-Carla had us both fooled? Maybe she was nothing more than a common gold digger, deeply embedded in the works of a conniving plot, a perfect setup; the ultimate sting.

But my instincts, for whatever they're worth, said otherwise. They told me her heart was good, and strong, and noble, beating to the rhythm of what she thought was right.

Far below, verdant jungle had replaced the desert. Rivers curled through forests like infinite racetracks. My guess was Guatemala or Honduras, where the Central Americas gave way to the South.

I glanced at Maria-Carla and had to smile. It was the irony of it all. I'd arrived in Mexico alone, seeing life through a dead man's eyes, in the sunset of my youth, just a little too old to keep hold of a young man's dream. Now, here I was on a private jet to Colombia. On a mission. A quest, if you will. This was far from the pursuit of a narcissistic goal. This was no Hollywood dream. This was riding into a secret fight, right into the danger zone, all for the forgotten sake of the right thing, like a modern-day Donkey Ho-Tay. Like the landscape below, I'd been brought back to life.

What could I do except enjoy the ride? I reclined my seat, kicked back, and relaxed. *Hasta luego*, Mexico. Next stop, Colombia.

13

An arrogant jolt of turbulence rattled the plane, finally waking the sleeping beauty that was Arturo. Maria-Carla gripped her arm rest, and looked around, on edge. I responded with a calm smile. Nothing to worry about. All part of the ride.

After checking his watch, Arturo struggled out of his seat, then came over and crouched beside me. "We land in ten minutes, *señor*. We will be met by a professional transporter."

We were to land in a hidden airfield, several hours drive from the Cali region. We would pass through what he referred to as *disputed territory*, hence the hiring of this transporter.

"Do not be surprised if he seems a little cold," added Arturo. "He assumes everyone is out to deceive him. It's how he survives."

"*Gracias*, Arturo. I'll be ready."

Any great actor knows that one must be meticulous in character study. The night before, I'd gone down a rabbit hole of research in the mansion's private library, reading various travel accounts from Latin America. I'd learned that Cali is located in the mountainous *Valle del Cauca* region of southwest Colombia. It's known as the city of eternal summer due to its tropical climate and proximity to the Pacific coastline.

Cali had a reputation as one of the most dangerous cities in Colombia, having endured decades of violence, right up until the present day.

Flying over the landscape, I noticed a beauty similar to Los Angeles. Both were cities built in the depths of a valley. But, while Los Angeles is a desert, Cali is a jungle.

The plane circled around to align with a small, concealed airstrip hidden by jungle terrain.

After a shaky landing, we rolled to a stop, smack

bang in the middle of the wilderness. There was no friendly word from the captain or farewell smile from a tired flight attendant. No grumpy old bastard trying to force his way through the aisle. There would be no customs line. No duty-free store to pick up a deal on cologne. We were invisible to the authorities; crossing international borders, our whereabouts unknown.

The exit door unfolded. I stepped out first, followed by Arturo, then Maria-Carla. I inhaled my first breath of the Colombian air, thick with forest mist. Calls of distant birds and other jungle creatures echoed from the surrounding wall of towering palm trees.

Three all-black Chevy Tahoes with tinted windows pulled up to park a few yards opposite the plane. The middle Tahoe crept toward us as a slim figure stepped out.

It was a man with a weathered face and a black leather coat. Not only was he pale, but scarily gaunt, so I nicknamed him *Skeleton Man*. He must've been boiling in that coat, but maybe skeletons don't over-heat. He spoke in a low, croaky voice.

"*Bienvenidos y buenos días, amigos. ¿Cómo estuvo tu vuelo?*"

Welcome and good morning, my friends. How was your flight?

"*Bien, bien amigo,*" said Arturo. "A little turbulence, but nothing unmanageable."

He cocked his head my way. "First time to Cali, *amigo?*"

I employed a little backstory work I'd hashed out the night before. "Not at all. Been coming here for years."

"From where?"

"Wherever I've been." Ambiguity always wins.

"And what is your favorite part of our beautiful city?"

I remembered a passage from my research the night before. I had read some random travel blog, the *Gringo Chronicles,* or something. "*Rio Pance,*" I said.

"Ah yes, a magical place. What impressed you the most?"

The writer had lazily alluded to some *undefinable feeling in the air*. Easy to plagiarize. "Oh, you know. Just the undefinable feeling in the air."

The Skeleton Man squinted. "The feeling in the air? That's very unspecific."

"*Señor*. Listen. I'd love to stand here and reminisce, but my team and I have places to be. And you know as well as I do, it isn't safe to stay so still. Not around these parts. Besides—"

I motioned to Maria-Carla.

"*Señora* Flores doesn't like to be kept waiting while you and I keep on about feelings in the air. Right, *Señora*?"

Maria-Carla gave me an icy glare. "I'm not bothered."

I leaned in and whispered to Skeleton Man. "That means she's bothered."

He maintained his stare for a few long moments before a slow grin revealed a nasty set of teeth. "*Entonces, vamos.*"

So, let's go.

He motioned us to the Tahoes. Two small men with dark suits and aggressive faces stepped out and opened our doors. They offered no greeting and seemed more robot than human. I dubbed them *Robot One* and *Robot Two*.

Maria-Carla and I were in the middle car of the three-vehicle convoy. Arturo rode in the front Tahoe with Skeleton Man.

I quietly asked Maria-Carla if she was mad at me. She whipped her head around.

"I don't like to be kept waiting? What the hell was that?"

I channeled a suave, devil-may-care approach, like a charismatic detective from an eighties cop show.

Those guys never really seemed worried, always making wisecracks in the face of menace.

"We can't show weakness. It was necessary."

"What's necessary is for you to not do anything stupid. I know *El Flamingo* likes to play by his own rules, but when you're with me, you play by mine. I'm the boss now. *¿Me entiendes?*"

You understand me?

I won't lie. Her words sent a sudden quiver of arousal all over me. For a second, I was reduced to no more than a big dumb *gringo* without a hope in hell of forming a sentence.

"*Te entiendo,*" I finally managed.

"*Muy bien.* And if shit hits the fan, don't do anything stupid."

"Consider it a mental note taken, boss."

She half-scowled, then turned away. If shit did hit the fan, I'd have to improvise. So far, I was going with plan A, which was to simply hope everything went smoothly. Plan B was yet to be devised.

For the next hour, we endured a bumpy ride along a dirt track that eventually merged onto an eerie mountain freeway. Rainforest mist distorted the view. We picked up speed, zooming around corners, swerving the cracks and dips of the beaten-down road.

Tension stiffened the air. Traffic was scarce. The robots would trade serious looks every so often. I remembered Arturo's words: "In Cali, there is always a threat."

As the Tahoes pushed through the thickening mist, some kind of a sixth sense told me things weren't quite right.

I looked at Maria-Carla. "Does something feel a little off to you?"

Almost right on cue, the front Tahoe braked.

Robot One said something to Robot Two. Maria-Carla edged forward to listen.

"What did they say?"

"That we shouldn't be stopping here."

Robot One's phone buzzed. He answered halfway through the first ring.

"*No,*" he said. "*No. No. Claro.*"

He pulled out a pistol from his jacket pocket. Robot Two followed his lead. As the mist began to clear, a shadow passed over Maria-Carla's face.

"*Mierda,*" she said.

Blocking our path was a military jeep, a green two-door with an open-air trailer. Old school, like you'd see in a 'Nam documentary. There were two in the front and three more in the trailer, all of them clutching AK47s. I didn't know much about guns, but I recognized those.

"*Bandas Criminales,*" said Maria-Carla. From her tone, I guessed she'd seen them before.

I'd read about these guys. Some called them rebels or guerrillas. Originally, they were born out of the demobilization of anti-government factions and paramilitary units engaged in a fifty-year-old war, but for gangs like these, it was not about politics. It was about money. More specifically, control of the coca-crops, drug-smuggling routes, and illegal gold mines. They weren't only drug-runners, but people smugglers, extortionists, and kidnappers, and they'd left a never-ending trail of bloodshed.

"Stay cool," I said to Maria-Carla in eighties cop-show lingo.

The two robots disembarked.

One of the bandits hopped out, his AK loose in his hand. He strolled toward us like he'd done this a thousand times before. The leader of the pack.

"Whatever they say, remain in the vehicle," said Maria-Carla.

"*Todos afuera!*" screamed the leader.

Everybody out!

"Do *not* get out of the vehicle!" Maria-Carla repeated. Spanish as fast as gunfire was exchanged. The robots shifted. The rest of the bandits jumped out and fixed their guns in our direction. The door of the lead Tahoe opened, and Arturo stepped out.

"What the hell is he doing?" I said aloud.

I had known this fella for only two days, yet here I was, watching him in the thick of danger, and I was damn worried about him. He seemed to be negotiating, making all sorts of diplomatic gestures, but the *bandas criminales* weren't having a bar of it.

Damnit Arturo!

I couldn't just leave him alone out there. There was something building inside me, but I wasn't sure what.

"Do *not* get out," said Maria-Carla again.

Robot One raised his voice.

The eyes of the bandits hardened. Trigger-fingers twitched.

Meanwhile, my acting instincts were kicking in—a physiological response. A Zen-like focus. My heartbeat slowed. I was no longer on edge, but on point. I knew what I had to do: *a monologue!*

The thespian's solo, if you will.

A great actor always keeps a back-pocket monologue handy at all times, in case of an unexpected audition. I'd performed a million of them before, in front of people who'd scared me a whole lot more than a pack of *bandas criminales*—L.A. producers.

Maria-Carla grabbed my wrist, sensing my compulsion to take action. "Do not get out of this *fucking* vehicle!"

I gave her devil-may-care; fifty percent grin, fifty percent gaze, and a hundred percent smolder.

"You have to trust me," I said. "This is what I do best."

I squeezed her hand and then, *yes*, I got out of the vehicle.

14

Outside, I heard only a cold, white silence. The sound of absolute focus.

I approached the commotion in no kind of hurry, shooting the cuffs of my suit jacket, a brazen smile on my face. Their AKs locked onto my skull in unison.

A great monologue always starts with a pre-beat, a brief moment before you begin speaking. I made a point of checking my watch. The guy who checks his watch is the guy in charge. I spread my hands in a feigned apology, like a CEO late to the board meeting.

"*Caballeros. No tenemos ningún problema aquí.*"

Gentleman. There doesn't have to be a problem here.

The leader stepped closer. He had a large facial tattoo and a smirk in his eyes.

"*¿No, gringo?*" he asked. "*¿Y por qué es eso?*"

And why is that?

"*Lo siento para mi Español, es horrible,*" I said. Self-deprecation. It's always charming.

I turned to Arturo. "Arturo, do me a solid and translate for me, would you?"

His eyebrows just about hit the heavens, but he found his composure. "*Si, señor.* I will do my best."

"Gentlemen," I began. "I understand that all of us here, in one way or another, are just trying to go about our business."

Arturo mirrored my tone in Spanish. Everyone looked a little confused.

"In English, we call that common ground. Is that something we can all agree on?"

They snickered. I didn't have their respect, but I had their attention.

"We're passing through your place of business. You feel a sense of territory, which is completely normal. I *get* that."

I offered a compassionate smile. "But here's the

thing. We have places to be, and very little time. Urgent business matters are at stake. Now, we ask for your cooperation in allowing us to pass without further hassle."

They sniggered again. A little less humor. A little more malice. I made a show of my disappointment.

"I can see there's been a misunderstanding. You're under the assumption that I'm having you on. Pulling your leg. Yanking your chain. So, I must clarify. Being that we are all business-minded, we can assume both parties have completed a level of risk assessment, in that we have identified what's known in the business world as the *economic hazards*."

Further confusion. Less patience. I kicked up the pace.

"Now, economic hazards are potential problems or obstacles that need to be identified well in advance, with preemptive solutions put in place. The situation we've all found ourselves in today, gentlemen, is a textbook example of an economic hazard."

The leader eyed me as Arturo translated. A rise to the challenge.

"*Para ti, si. Puto.*"

I pretended to be unfamiliar with the word.

"*Puto*? Arturo, what does '*puto*' mean?"

Arturo gulped and loosened his tie. "Ahh. It is not a nice word, *señor*."

"It's an insult?"

"*Si señor*. A bad insult."

I turned back to the leader. "You know, *amigo*, a baseless noun designed to evoke an emotional response from a potential foe is a sure revelation of your intellectual capabilities. Quite frankly, it's an amateur move. I thought we were all professionals here."

Slowly, the smirk rolled over. The guns cocked. I stepped closer.

"To further the extent of your unprofessionalism,

you've failed to identify a risk to yourself and your *compadres*."

I paused for effect before continuing.

"You, sir, are nothing but a common terrorist. Your business operates on the basis of fear. You may argue there is nothing for you to be afraid of. I would argue, however, that you are mistaken. I can see in your eyes that you are not afraid of me. That is a lapse in professional judgment."

I changed gears again, opting for a softer tone. Great actors are unpredictable.

"Tell me, by what name can I call you?"

He raised his chin and pumped his chest. "*El Guillotino.*"

"*El Guillotino*? Nice. Very evocative. Why do they call you *El Guillotino*?"

"*Porque tomo las cabezas de mis enemigos.*"

Because I take the heads of my enemies.

"Wow," I said. "That's a cool pseudonym, *amigo.*"

He nodded and seemed to appreciate the compliment. Maybe in another life, we could have been friends.

"I also have a pseudonym. One you may have heard of."

"*Si? Qué es?*"

I let the silence linger, then calmly said, "They call me...*El Flamingo.*"

The atmosphere turned upside down. The leader stepped back. His gang spread out. It was like a family day at the beach, when it's all fun and laughter, until someone sees a shark.

"Aha. I can see you've heard of me."

The leader shook his head. "*Mentira.*"

Arturo looked my way, sweat pouring from his forehead.

"He thinks you're lying, *señor.*"

I shook my head. "No, you don't. You'd like to *think* I'm lying, but you're really not sure. Now hear me! As

a consummate professional, I pride myself on prepa-
ration. Details. The little things you missed because
you're lazy."

Arturo maintained my quickening pace.

"I am never lazy. Not for a goddamn second. I did
the work. That's why I'm the best. You've heard of me,
but I've never heard of you."

He sought to speak, but I held up my palm.

"I'm not finished. Did you not think I would have
researched the route? That I wouldn't have planned
for obstacles? Did you not think I would have snipers?"

The bandits all peered toward the mountains like
deer at the detection of a predator. It all came down
to whether they believed me or not. I put the odds at
about fifty-fifty.

I raised my hand in the air, a signal to my imaginary
snipers. "This is your last chance, fellas. If I drop my
hand, each and every one of you gets a bullet between
the eyes."

They all boxed in together, back-to-back.

"Now drop your weapons. *¡Ahora!*"

Now!

As an actor, if you don't believe, then no one else
will. In that moment, I could truly see my snipers set
up in the hills, locked in, and ready to fire. Great actors
fool even themselves.

Slowly, the leader lowered his weapon and chucked
it aside.

The others followed suit.

I let out a breath and made a big deal out of waving
the imaginary snipers away.

"You made the right choice, *amigos*." I turned to the
robots. "Take their guns and shoot out their tires."

I turned toward the *bandas criminales* one final
time.

"You're all young men. There is still time. I understand you probably come from less-than-privileged

backgrounds, where opportunities for a better path are few and far between. I'm in no position to give you a moral sermon. But I know we have a daily choice between the good, the bad, and the cowardly. Think long and hard. You seem like tough guys. Like hard men. I'm sure you are, but this whole thing you got going on right here? It's the easy way out. Using violence as a way to take what's not yours? It's a coward's move. Real tough guys do a little something called *the right thing*. It may not be easy, but I urge you all to give it a try. And don't use words like *puto,* because what is it, Mr. *Guillotino?*"

"*No profesional,*" he said, his eyes glued to the ground.

There you have it—*El Flamingo*: Full-time assassin, part-time philosopher.

Arturo sent them on their way. I turned around to get back in the Tahoe and saw Maria-Carla, who had been standing right behind me. At some point during my theatrics, she must have disembarked the vehicle. I couldn't tell if she was impressed, or furious, or both.

"What the hell was that?" she demanded.

I escorted her back to the car and opened her door. "I already told you," I said. "It was what I do best."

15

Two hours later, we arrived in Cali, where the rugged metropolis was wide awake. Horns honked, voices yelled, and the tunes of distant salsa songs rang out from a maze of busy breakfast joints. I glimpsed a thousand lives, all moving with a sense of purpose. A convolution of suited office workers, bare-chested street salesmen, and striding students formed a harmonious hustle and bustle. It was easy to see this city had soul.

We passed historical monuments, colonial housing, and hotels that might've been modern in the 1970s. At a traffic light, a young kid backflipped over the hood of a car to the beat of reggaeton, and the driver handed him a couple of coins. Painted on the side of an abandoned building was a jaguar, roaring out across the stone jungle.

"We're close to *El Peñon*," said Maria-Carla. "The hotel is nearby."

It was nearing nine, and the sun was already high above the heights of the eastern valley. The aromas of fresh coffee traveling from street corner cafés commanded me to find a cup as soon as possible. Hell, even the robots looked like they needed their batteries recharged.

I reflected on how the previous events had unfolded. I had come face-to-face with death, but my acting skills had swooped in and saved me. Who would've thought acting was a superpower?

I reminded myself to be humble. Don't go thinking you're bulletproof, Galloway. Nothing gets you killed like a Hollywood ego.

We pulled up to a hotel that must have been thirty floors high. Written in a vintage font above the entrance doors was *La Vela de Cali.*

The Candle of Cali.

A beaming Arturo hopped out of the front Tahoe. "Genius, *señor*. Genius!"

"Your translations were impeccable," I said. "Team effort all around."

The Skeleton Man appeared with a grim frown. "Well, *amigos*, here we are."

"Thanks for the ride."

"You know," he said, "we appreciated your theatrics, but we had the situation under control."

The bastard hadn't even left his vehicle.

"So I saw. You really went above and beyond."

"And is it true what you said? Are you the real... *Flamingo*?"

"Of course not. Those guys would believe anything. I could have said I was Zorro."

His eyes sharpened. "That's exactly the kind of thing that *El Flamingo* would say."

"I wouldn't know," I smiled. "I am not him, and he is not I."

He stared hard, clearly unsatisfied.

"Take good care. I hope your business here goes as planned."

"You and me both. Now giddy up, Tornado."

"Excuse me?"

"It's another Zorro reference, meaning feel free to hit the road."

With a bewildered shake of his head, he climbed back into his Tahoe, as he and his convoy of robots departed.

A large concierge team escorted us through the revolving doors into the lobby. It was a luxury hotel in a retro kind of a way: gold-tiled floors, sunset paintings, and an artificial waterfall in the center. At the hotel bar, a young pianist played notes of soft Latin jazz, smiling at passing guests. I wondered if he was one of Diego's spies. Musically gifted, sure, but a spy, nonetheless.

While Arturo handled the check-in process, I scoped out the interior. I may have saved the day once already, but that didn't mean I could kick back and switch off. Curious eyes from the indoor balconies above peered down at the new arrivals. Innocent guests curious to people-watch, most likely, but maybe not. I stared back, sternly, just to let them know I was aware, should they too, be spies.

"Impressed?" asked Maria-Carla.

"Just watching out for the ones watching us."

One of the most important rules of the actor's handbook is, "It's not what *you* would do. It's what your character would do."

What would *El Flamingo* do? He would remain calm, yet on high alert, scoping for threats, memorizing details; eyes in the back of his fedora-covered head. All while looking like he hadn't a care in the world.

Diego had said *La Vela de Cali* was the best and most secure hotel in the region. Our arrival was highly secretive. His mistrust of his employees ran so deep that he'd created aliases for each of us. It was easy to feel safe now that we were encircled by tourists and hospitality staff, but it was all smoke and mirrors. Security is mere illusion.

"Cali is just like Mexico," Diego had said. "Everything is fine, until it's not fine."

The check-in completed, a pair of bell boys stacked our bags and led us into the elevator and up to our floor. We stepped into a long hallway of red-checkered carpet. We arrived at our room, then Arturo sent them on their way with a hefty tip. He held an electronic sensor card to the door. The lock made a sound like R2D2, then popped open.

It was the goddamn presidential suite!

A floor-to-ceiling window circled the room in a panoramic curve, the view stretching from the city to the valley mountains. White canopy curtains hovered over a bed the size of a boxing ring. The madman inside me imagined a pillow fight with Maria-Carla, clothing-optional, but I refrained from suggesting it. You have to time these things right, or God forbid, Arturo might want to join in.

Arturo pulled open a sliding door to reveal a second king-sized bedroom replete with its own ensuite bathroom.

"These are your quarters, *señor*. I will be in a room across the hall. The boss wants you to be closest to Maria-Carla, in case of any trouble."

"Understood," I said, in the most businesslike tone I could muster. "It's for the best."

Arturo looked at his watch. "Now, I must go. I have a series of security checks I must conduct."

"Security checks?"

He almost winked. "Security checks."

Could it be he was sneaking off for a secret liaison? The mysterious Arturo: part-time butler, international womanizer.

He looked around at the walls like the whole place could be a trap.

"Remember. We never know who may be listening."

I nodded sincerely. "We never know."

He gave me a firm grasp on the shoulder, then left. And just like that, Maria-Carla and I were alone in the suite. *Ay, caramba!*

16

Maria-Carla pulled out her phone and said, "I need to make a call."

Taking this clear cue for me to leave the room, I entered my adjoining quarters. After the eventful morning, I figured it was time for a change of clothes. Inside my travel bag were a couple of plain white tees, some collared shirts, a pair of jeans, a selection of briefs and socks, and a shaving kit. Beneath all that was something else. A large, firm object, enclosed in a black leather holster. I picked it up and gently removed the weapon, a silver pistol with a hardwood grip. Engraved in simple font along the inner side of the barrel were the words, *Smith & Wesson*.

I'd fired prop guns. They may look real from a distance, but in your hand, you can tell they're nothing but a stage gimmick.

This was different. You could sense the power in its icy weight. I tried to picture how I would go about actually using it on a living being. Aiming at their head, their eyes glued to mine, urgently willing me to let them live, and then squeezing the trigger. I shuddered at the image and buried the gun back in the bag.

"It's strange," said a voice from behind.

Maria-Carla stood in the doorway. She'd changed into a white linen dress that hung loosely over her shoulders, her breasts threatening to pounce out at me any second. Eyes on her eyes, I told myself. You are *El Flamingo*: Full-time assassin, consummate gentleman.

"What is?" I asked.

"The notorious *El Flamingo* acting a stranger to the tools of his trade."

Shit! How long had she been there? Had she watched me analyze the pistol like a guy who'd never touched a weapon before? I'd forgotten another fundamental rule in the actor's handbook: *Never break character. Even when no one is looking.* I attempted to cover up the error with an improvised babble of idiocy.

"Sometimes, Maria-Carla, I wish I *was* a stranger to these wretched things. I've been on both sides of them. I've squeezed the trigger. I've stared down the barrel. I've cheated death myself, and I've introduced it to others. I've seen enough guns in my time never to take their power for granted."

She mockingly put her hand on her hip.

"The power to take away life."

"A power none of us should have."

"Interesting, considering it is coming from a man who uses that power to make his living."

I gazed to the mountain valley like a character out of the Old West, a burdened ranger clinging to the last of his soul, plagued by the countless lives he'd been forced to take over a career of constant war.

"These days, killing is too easy. There was a time when man's only weapon was his bare hands. To kill a man, you killed him fairly; may the stronger man survive. But, our bare hands became a rock, and the rock became a blade. Then came the gun. A life removed with just the simple squeeze of a trigger. That's when it all really went south."

"I can see you are a deep thinker," said Maria-Carla.

"Among the deepest."

"Who knew a typesetting salesman could be so philosophical."

"Let me tell you. This 'typesetting' business may be how I make my living," I said, "But sleeping at night is a whole 'nother story."

She surveyed me as I hoped my tortured act had left her convinced. Whoever she was, she was a hard woman to read.

"I wouldn't have thought a man like you would have

such a heavy heart. Most men in your line of work have no conscience. Many even *like* what they do."

I offered no response. Great acting requires a little mystery. The audience should be in the palm of the actor's hand, longing to know what he's thinking.

Maria-Carla turned around and said, "I'm going to take a bath now."

"Excuse me?"

"I said I'm going to take a bath."

"A bath?"

"Yes. A bath."

She looked back, gauging my reaction. Was this an *invitation*?

"Okay. Well...I guess—"

"That wasn't an invitation," she said, quite possibly reading my mind.

"Of course not. I didn't take it that way," I stuttered, both of us knowing full-well I'd taken in that way.

"Of course, you didn't. As you said, you're a professional."

"Professionalism is all I know."

"*Muy bien.* Well, I'd appreciate some privacy. So...."

I had an urge to jump head-first out the window just so I'd never again have to look her in the eye.

"Sure thing," I said. "In that case, I'll just go for a wander. See the sights."

"Okay. I'll see you in the afternoon.... And take care out there."

I traded the suit for a pair of light denim jeans and a creme shirt, then I was out the door and down the elevator. Strolling through the lobby, my phone buzzed. Tommy. Again! A video call this time. Noting the multiple security cameras fixed in each corner, I kept the phone low and concealed.

There was Tommy's greasy face staring up at me through the desperate eyes of a showbiz hustler. This guy was about as L.A as it got.

"Tommy, it's not a good time."

"Galloway! Christ's sake. Where the hell are ya? Ya still in Mexico?"

"Just breathe, Tommy. I'm in Colombia."

He leaned back in his swivel chair and threw his hands in the air.

"Colombia now? Jesus! What the hell are ya doing down there? Learning the fuckin' salsa?"

"There's no time to explain. But it's bigger than salsa."

"Listen, Galloway. You need to know. You've lost your goddamn mind, but that's alright. Great actors lose their minds all the time. That's why ya' got an agent. It's where I come swooping in to wipe everyone's ass."

"Tommy, no one's asking you to wipe anyone's ass. Focus on your own ass."

"Don't you get it, Galloway? You *are* my ass! An ass that needs to be back in L.A where you fuckin' belong!

"Tommy—"

"You wanna learn salsa? They got salsa here! I'll even take the class with you if I gotta!"

"Tommy. I can't leave Colombia right now."

He stuck his index finger into the camera.

"Now don't make me come down there! I got you something big—"

Before he could finish his sentence, the phone cut out. Dead battery.

I couldn't help but wonder what the hell that damn Tommy was going to say, but nothing could be done about that right now, so I set out as planned.

Hitting the streets solo, I had to keep a low profile.

They say, in Cali, there is safety in movement. Stay too still, and you could become a target. With my white skin and sandy-blonde hair, I was the strutting embodiment of the naïve American. So I got a wriggle on.

I started up a graffiti-clad street, keeping my expression neutral, with a hint of self-assurance, like I'd been here a while. Just another Cali local, a fish in familiar waters, floating along streets I knew like the back of my hand. I had my cover story down. If anyone asked what brought me to town, I would say I was a lone travel writer who'd come to investigate the salsa capital of the world.

I soon found myself in a colonial neighborhood called *San Antonio* that smelled like flowers and concrete. Built on a steep incline, its narrow streets were decorated with colorful townhouses that looked unchanged since the Spanish arrived.

Hole-in-the-wall bars and underground restaurants were beautifully concealed in the nooks and crannies of urbanization; easily missed if you weren't curious.

I passed a two-story house painted blue and yellow. A small woman, who could have been a hundred-and-sixty years old, spotted me strolling along from her tiny balcony.

"*Café!*" she yelled. Her smile displayed a row of terrible teeth, but her eyes were a window to a kind soul. I respected her saleswoman-ship.

"*Si,*" I called back. "*Café. Por favor.*"

The coffee shop seemed to double as the living room in the off hours. There was only one small table that wobbled about as much as the old gal herself.

I watched her grind the dark beans finely and stir them into a pot of boiling water, letting them brew for several minutes before filtering it through an old-fashioned drip-cloth, holding back each grain, allowing the liquid to flow like a sacred river of caffeine.

She brought me the coffee in a little wooden cup and observed me take the first sip. It was smooth, but strong, offering notes of chocolate brownie and almonds. I understood why she used the drip cloth method; centuries old, but there's no test like time.

"*¿Rico, no?*"

Delicious, no?

"*Increíble,*" I confirmed.

She giggled at what I guessed was my shocking pronunciation, then waddled on back to the kitchen. *El Flamingo: He makes the ladies smile.*

As it always does, the coffee began to raise my overall level of intelligence. A focus came over me. The embarrassment of the bath incident had passed, at least until I next saw Maria-Carla. I had a window of time alone, and the question was how it could best be used. What I needed most was more information. Access to a resource that could tell me about anyone and anything at any time. Enter the Internet.

The computers for guest use back at the hotel weren't an option. Too many cameras, too much attention. With my phone battery dead, I would have to go old school. I wondered if they still had Internet cafes in Cali.

The old gal waddled back over and refilled my cup, her grin once again exposing the extent of her orthodontic catastrophe. It was a knowing smile, like she knew I was hiding something, but my secret would be safe with her. Perhaps she knew all. Maybe she was God Herself.

I paid for the coffee, plus a decent tip. She mumbled something in Spanish which was hard to understand, but I think she said that she hoped I would find what I was searching for. I said *muchas gracias*, then set off for *El Centro*.

17

El Centro by car was one thing, but by foot, it was a whole other experience. When we'd arrived that morning, the chaotic beauty of the place had been a dancing image, a filmic world seen through a car window. This time, I, myself, was a facet of the scene. I drew looks at every turn; friendly smiles, curious glances. A wandering tourist reeking of Western privilege. I passed a series of historic buildings—a university campus, an eighteenth-century theatre, and a seventeenth-century church. Then, I was into *el corazón de Cali*.

Before long, I began to experience a sensory overload in the thick of such close-quarters immersion. I weaved through hustling crowds and layers of noise from empanada stands, bootleg clothing stalls, and homemade-jewelry stores.

I stopped for a break at a small fruit and vegetable market. There was no air conditioning, but old fans rattled up some kind of a breeze. Near the checkout was a beaten-down ATM. I inserted my credit card, which I'd damn near maxed out during my escape from L.A. Miraculously, it worked and spat out a wad of pesos.

I bought a banana and a bottle of water and asked the girl at the checkout where I could find the nearest Internet cafe. She pointed across the road to an indoor market.

Halfway along a stretch of stores selling cheap blue jeans and knockoff Ray-Bans, I came to a tiny stairway leading underground. Hand-lettered on a cut-out sign was "*Café Internet.*"

A thin boy of about sixteen sat behind a cluttered desk, his eyes fixed on a Rubik's cube. He had three sides completed and was on his way to a fourth. Better than I'd ever done. When he looked up, he seemed surprised.

"*Hola señor. ¿Cómo puedo ayudarte?*"

How can I help?

"*Buenos días. Necesito una hora, por favor.*"

I need one hour, please.

"*Claro,*" he said.

He pointed to a computer near the back. There were only a couple of people in the place—a kid playing an online shoot-'em-up game and a couple of teenage girls watching a makeup tutorial.

I sat down at a dusty PC from the early 2000s, logged on, and entered my first search: "Diego Flores."

First to appear was a series of images of the actor who'd portrayed him in the TV adaptation, along with magazine interviews and links to the trailer. It was a high-budget, sensationalist soap opera that made a big deal of glorifying the cartel lifestyle. Images of the real Diego Flores were few and far between. A few search pages in, however, I came across an investigative piece on an independent Mexican news site. The home page said they prided themselves on maintaining a standard of "honest, objective, and un-corruptible journalism."

The piece was a few years old, written by a journalist named Carmen Gonzalez, focusing on the timeline of Diego's suspected crimes. A low-resolution photo showed a young Diego Flores in a dark suit, standing at the back of a group of older, heavy-set men. He appeared young and hungry, his eyes full of ambition, a sharp contrast to the eyes of defeated cynicism I looked into this morning. The caption read, "Guadalajara, 1999." The article discussed numerous crimes he was believed to have been connected to: political assassinations, kidnappings, and his supposed involvement with a group of clandestine graves.

Another photo showed a federal police captain who'd vowed not to back down after making a trail of high-profile arrests that targeted key players within Diego's chain of command. One day, he and his wife had been seized from their home by masked men. The captain and his wife were never found.

Additional scrolling brought me to a more recent photo of Diego standing before an expensive casket, his head held low. Beside him was a Catholic priest reading from the Bible.

Black shades masked his eyes, and his hands were tucked into the pockets of a long, dark coat. This time, he was at the front of the crowd. Other suited men gathered around, but space was given—respect; hierarchical superiority.

The story said the funeral was for a man with organized crime affiliations who'd been taken from his front porch one night and dumped back the following day as a headless corpse. No arrests had been made. The only suspect in the case was Diego Flores himself, the same man pictured at the center of the mourning. No legal action had been taken. After cocaine had been seized in tunnels he'd built under the Texas border, Diego was now deemed an international criminal.

Carmen Gonzalez, the reporter, had been in the midst of a widespread investigative piece, holding the hope of exposing Flores and the army of corrupt officials, politicians, police, and military personnel who enabled his empire. However, shortly after her work was published, she, too, had disappeared. The entire publication had shut down after the managing editor stated he had failed his staff by not protecting them. Three months later, he shot himself.

I considered the things Diego Flores had done—the evil he had perpetrated. The thing is, I would have felt fear if it wasn't for my rage. His tortured, misunderstood-father act, demonstrated at his daughter's wedding, had lost its illusion. He was a violent, cruel-hearted son-of-a-bitch, and I'd be damned if I'd let him use me for his wicked deeds. To hell with him. *El Flamingo* was his own man, and *El Flamingo* would go his own way.

I searched "Maria-Carla Flores."

It returned a useless, infinite list of all the Maria-Carlas in the world.

I typed instead, "wife of Diego Flores." Mostly, it brought up posts from crazed women infatuated with the idea of being loved by a gangster. Buried among them, however, was a slightly pixelated image of Diego opening the passenger door of a luxury car. I enlarged the image. On closer inspection, you could make out the shape of a woman about to step out of the car. I instantly recognized the waist-length hair and the angle at which she held her head. The photo took me to an article called, "The Woman Behind El Buitre."

The story was written by an amateur true-crime writer named Otto Peach. Beside the title was a headshot of Peach, an out-of-shape man in his sixties. His jaw was clenched and his eyes were fixed in a determinedly inquisitive gaze.

To Peach's credit, the article wasn't half bad. It was highly speculative, but claiming to have a source in a law-enforcement agency, he wrote that the woman behind Diego Flores was the key to his operations. Nothing was known about her identity, her whereabouts, or her background, however. Peach wrote that the FBI had a strong interest in her, and believed that if they couldn't find Flores, she was their next best target. Peach said he'd reached out to the CIA, who were also thought to be hunting Flores, but they'd never acknowledged his query. After seeing his headshot, I could understand why.

Across the room, the kid playing the shoot-'em-up game let out a victorious shriek that startled both the makeup girls and myself. I guess he was winning.

I refocused, and searched "Juan Moreno." It returned hundreds of images of a man in his forties with a solid frame and impassioned eyes. Since his late twenties, he'd been leading anti-corruption rallies around the

Valle del Cauca region as well as all of Colombia.
Before that, he'd served in the army, where he'd been
a captain of a specialized unit designed to investigate
war crimes and human rights violations committed by
paramilitary units. I clicked on a YouTube video of an
interview he'd done with a local news station. The title
was *"Juan Moreno: ¿El próximo presidente de Colombia?"* I adjusted the subtitles to English.

"The economy is broken. The cost of living is rising,
while the quality of life is sinking. Corruption is our
shadow. Juan Moreno, what is your plan for the future
of Colombia?" the narrator asked.

Moreno's responses were calm and considered, with
an undercurrent of defiance in his voice.

"Colombia is my heart. It always will be. But there
is a cancer here. All of my life I saw my people punished for doing the right thing. They die for taking a
stand. People who put their trust in the powers that
be—only to be put on their backs. And yet, they keep
fighting. Yes. There are snakes among us. Dirty politicians. Dirty cops. Dirty leaders. But right alongside,
right in the fight, are the ones who refuse to turn their
backs."

Moreno paused, wiped a bead of sweat, then smiled.
"I walk the streets and I see humanity. I see hustle,
grit, and compassion. I see the strength to stay in this
brawl. I believe the fight is now with ourselves more
than anyone. The cancer that kills us is not the corruption. It's not the violence. It's not the blood. What kills
us is believing that the fight is over."

The audience erupted and I was beginning to see
why he was the people's champ.

"But we are not going to let that happen! We
are going to fight. Not with hate or guns, but with
choice. We will fight with knowledge. We will fight
with education. We will fight for the sake of what
is right because justice is contagious. Justice breeds

hope. We are not alone. We will not be scared. We will be strong. Because, most of all, we will be fighting together."

A series of chills flew down my back. You had to hand it to Moreno. The man knew how to win over a crowd.

It was nearing midday, so I thought I better head back to the hotel so not to arouse suspicion in Maria-Carla. Before I returned, there was one last thing I wanted to search.

"*El Flamingo.*"

It came back with cocktail bars, restaurants, dancing events, strip clubs, festivals, and of course, flamingo sanctuaries.

I tried "*El Flamingo*—person."

Not much appeared other than people taking selfies standing among flamingos in the wild.

I added several other variants to this search: "hitman," "contract killer," "assassin," "*sicario.*"

But *nada.* Nothing at all. Diego was right. To the world, *El Flamingo* did not exist.

I paid the boy at the desk and re-entered the crowded marketplace, fighting my way through its charming shambles. It would be roughly a half-hour walk back to the hotel in the more tranquil suburb of El Peñon. Surely Maria-Carla would be out of the bath by now. Right?

I came to an overpass bridge. From across the other side of the busy road, a young mother and her son walked hand in hand, heading in the opposite direction, toward *El Centro.* The child watched me with wide, searching eyes. To my amazement, he called across the speeding cars in English:

"You lost, *gringo?*"

His mother kept hold of his hand and seemed oblivious to our exchange.

"*No. No estoy perdido.* But *gracias, amigo,*" I called back.

With a broad smile, the boy called out once more, like no matter what I told him, he was sure of what he saw.

"You lost, *gringo.*"

I watched the boy and his mother become tiny shapes in the distance. The sun shone across the urban landscape as old cars and loud scooters hurtled by. I was nothing more than an invisible man in a foreign land.

A sudden presence roused me from my introspection when an all-black BMW pulled up to the curb. Three people stepped out, quickly surrounding me and blocking all possible escape paths. They wore suits, sunglasses, and expressions that said they came for people all the time, and today they were coming for me. On the left was a large dark-skinned man with a bald head and monstrous shoulders. On the right was a thick-set white dude with a long goatee that should have been shaved off for good months ago. In the middle was a coffee-skinned woman with a buzz cut and a scowl. The trio looked as out of place in Cali as I did, and I would bet they were American. The shoulders guy opened the door for me; polite, for a broad-daylight abduction. The woman in the middle stepped forward and pulled back her jacket to reveal a gun strapped to her waist.

"*El Flamingo,*" she said. "It's time we talked."

18

My eyes were open, but all was dark. They'd tossed me into the Beemer, cuffed my hands, and pulled a black bag over my head. "You know the drill," they'd said.

I did?

Breathe deep and roll with it, I told myself. You're *El Flamingo,* and *El Flamingo* would know the drill.

I might have been a little more fearful, but my near-death encounter with the *bandas criminales* had me feeling like I could handle the whole underworld with nothing but absolute self-belief. Dark suits weren't as scary as facial tattoos. Stupid, maybe, but caution had been chucked to the wind a long time ago.

We drove for maybe an hour, picking up speed on flatter roads, a tell that we had left the city and were headed for the rural outskirts. Who were these guys? They definitely had some kind of an *agency* feel. Maybe FBI or DEA. Maybe something a little more secretive.

We came to a stop. I heard somebody get out of the car, followed by the opening of a rusty gate, then we drove up some kind of bumpy, gravel road as the smell of grass and clean air came through the windows. Some kind of farm, I guessed.

They escorted me out of the BMW and inside onto creaky floorboards. The dusty scent suggested un-inhabitance; abandonment; isolation. A space chosen for a sole purpose—away from the eyes and ears of possible witnesses.

I was taken down a flight of narrow stairs, steered by strong hands digging into my arms. They shoved me down onto a rickety chair and tied my hands behind me. I thought a wisecrack might help ease the tension.

"If this is some kind of BDSM thing you got going here, I'm gonna need more information."

"Shut the fuck up."

"Then I don't consent."

"Noted, asshole."

"Seriously, if I knew the safety word, I would've said it by now."

A door slammed shut, and I was left alone in the heat and the silence.

Minutes, or maybe hours, or maybe days went by as a wrestling match between my rage and my boredom set in. So this was to be what, an interrogation? A torture session? An execution? All three in succession? Bastards!

The thing was, sitting here in this chair felt oddly familiar. I'd been here before, at least in my imagination.

It was maybe ten years ago, back in a town called L.A. I was waiting my turn in a shitty audition studio somewhere in the backstreets of West Hollywood. At the time I had no agent, but I'd managed to lie my way in after I'd heard talk of an action flick casting from some loud-talking champ in my acting class.

I was up for the role of a soldier who gets captured in the Afghanistan desert and is interrogated by a faction of the Taliban.

Before a panel of two producers and one director, I'd fallen into character. I was focused, still, and ready to nail the scene. I could feel the burn of my battle wounds and the scorch of the Middle Eastern sun. I was about to hit them with the painfully written opening line of the monologue: "You bastards think I'll talk? I don't think so. I'm too American to break."

"And...whenever you're ready," said a producer, sounding sick of me already. Another producer was scrolling through his phone, resting his chin in his palm. Meanwhile, the director just stared through his spectacles with a blank frown, like I might as well have been empty space.

I spat out my first line like a wad of fresh blood.

"You assholes think I'll talk? I don't think so. I'm too American to break!"

The first producer sighed. The other one stayed on his phone. The director said, "I'm gonna stop you there."

"Okay," I said. "You wanna get a closer frame?"

"No. I think I've seen enough."

"Enough? I just started."

"Exactly."

A cocktail of embarrassment and anger swirled in my stomach.

"Listen. You wanna give me some direction, I can take it. You want less of this or more of that, I'll make the adjustment. Maybe I was too subtle? Or maybe you want a bigger choice? What was the problem?"

The director shrugged and said, "I just don't believe you."

To an actor, being told you weren't believable is like being castrated in front of your ex-girlfriends, all of them watching from a close-in grandstand.

"You didn't believe me?"

"I didn't see anything real."

"You didn't see anything...*REAL?*"

"Nada."

With the bridge already burning, I thought I might as well watch it explode. "Then maybe you should get some thicker fuckin' glasses."

They gasped as the director lowered his spectacles. "Excuse me?"

"You know what the problem is with this town? You lay your heart on the fucking line, and all you get back is a lump of shit."

I walked up to their table and flipped all their papers into the air. They reared back in shock.

"I'm calling the police!" said the director.

"Go ahead," I said. "Tell them there's been a homicide. Tell them the art of acting is dead."

It was a really corny line, but what the hell. I stormed out and stomped to my car. I started the engine and was about to speed off when a guy jumped in front of the car. He wore a cheap mustard-colored suit and a fake Armani watch.

"Stop right there!" he shouted.

"Get outta the way, asshole!"

"I can't do that. Not until you tell me your name."

"Lou fucking Galloway," I screamed. "Now move!"

"Lou Galloway," the guy repeated to himself, as if he liked the cut of its jib. He mopped a bead of sweat from his brow with a yellowing pocket square. "Well, Lou Galloway, that was the greatest fuckin' thing I've ever heard."

I put on the hand brake. "Excuse me?"

"Passion, kid. The kind that only comes along once in a lifetime."

"You heard all that?"

"You bet your Emmy/Oscar-winning asshole I did. Been waitin' a long time to hear something like that."

Slowly, as if trying to tame a wild horse, the guy edged around to the passenger side and got into the car.

"I'm in the entertainment business." To me, this sounded like he was saying he worked in porn.

"What exactly do you do?" I asked.

"I manage talent."

That definitely sounded like porn.

"That sounds like you work in porn," I said aloud.

"I don't work in porn! I manage *real* talent."

"Sure."

"Thing about managing talent is, you gotta find it first."

"Okay."

"After witnessing that, I don't gotta look no further."

"Witnessing what?"

"The last guy in Hollywood with a little fire inside."

He reached into his jacket pocket and pulled out a rumpled business card. "The name's Tommy Blue.

Hollywood agent. Something tells me you're lookin' for representation."

We looked at each other for a spell, like two stray cats in a downtown alley.

"You sure you don't work in porn?"

"Not so far. And I hope to keep it that way."

"Then yeah, I'm looking for representation."

Tommy offered his hand.

"You know what? I think you're gonna be a star. I think you and I are gonna do something big in this world. Something *real* big."

And for the first time in forever, someone believed in me. We both looked ahead to the hazy metropolis, where the sun blazed behind a wall of California smog.

"You know kid, there's a lot of smog over this town," said Tommy, "but if you know where to search, the sun will shine through."

"Then let's get searching."

We set off for the skyline, as if chasing a sunset that couldn't be caught, plotting and scheming about all the ways we could crack the Hollywood code and hustle our dreams into existence. What a long time ago that was.

19

An indeterminable chunk of time later, the door opened and closed as footsteps entered the room. Someone removed the bag from my head. I now saw I was in a ratty, underground basement with mold on the walls and dirt coming up through the floorboard cracks.

A single light bulb hung from the ceiling and a tripod stood in the corner. Across from me was a small chair and table. Classic. An interrogation room if ever I saw one.

The buzz-cut woman strolled into my line of sight and tossed the face-bag in the corner. She sat on the empty chair and leaned back, like we had all the time in the world to get to know each other. There was a black pen in her hand, but curiously, no paper.

I was dizzy, exhausted, and unbearably thirsty, but before I requested a soda, I needed to know the time. "What hour is it?" I asked. "What's the date? How many days has it been?"

The buzz-cut woman checked her watch. "About forty-five minutes."

Well.... That was embarrassing.

"My name is Erica," she said. "I'll ask only one thing of you, which is that you be honest."

Definitely American. Educated. Agency.

"My word is my bond," I replied, preparing to continue my elaborate lie.

Erica smiled, crossed her legs, and said, "We know who you are. In fact, we know *exactly* who you are."

From her jacket, she pulled out something I should've thrown away the second I decided to accept this role— my damned wallet. I gave myself a rousing welcome to the Hall of Fame for Utter Morons.

"We found this on your person," she said.

I said nothing.

She slipped the license out and looked it over with a smirk. "Lou Galloway."

With my pulse galloping, I realized my fate. I'd been caught in the trap of my own lies. Just as I was truly settling into my character, the game was up. It was time to spill the beans, to admit I was nothing but a failed actor caught up in a plot far out of my depth. I exhaled, trying to figure out where the hell to begin. Mexico? The fedora? The wedding? But just as I opened my mouth, Erica spoke again. "It's one hell of a cover."

I closed my mouth.

"Not to mention, one of the best fake identifications I've ever seen."

"Excuse me?"

"Don't fuck with us, *Lou Galloway*." She made a big deal of holding up her fingers, putting air quotes around my name. "We did our homework. You devised an elaborate backstory. A struggling actor living in Los Angeles with a handful of bullshit credits to his name. In fact, it's *almost* believable. 'Lou Galloway' even *sounds* like an L.A. fuck-up."

That last part really hurt.

"You had a stack of shitty headshots done," she went on. "Signed up to a bunch of bullshit casting websites. Even joined the books of some d-grade talent agent."

Tommy would've hated her.

"You really went all out, didn't you?"

If I wasn't mistaken, it seemed this highly professional black ops agent genuinely believed that Lou Galloway was a false identity I'd somehow created in order to remain hidden. I fell back on the fundamentals.

"I'm not sure I follow."

"Oh, you follow, alright. Now quit jerking us off."

"I'm not jerking you, or anyone, off."

She slammed her fist on the table. "Cut the shit, Operative Eighty-One."

Operative Eighty-One?

She flicked the license to the other side of the room.

"You and your pseudonyms. Lou Galloway is just another cute misdirect to who you really are, no different to this '*El Flamingo*' nonsense. Typical rogue mindset. You think you're smarter than the ones who trained you. And maybe, for a time, you *were*. But times change."

And so, once again, the plot thickens. *A rogue mindset?* Deeply perplexing, yes, but acting-wise, it was great news. The show had to go on. I fell back into character and shoved the rearing head of Lou Galloway back into the trenches. Somehow, I'd become an utterly unreadable man, all down to the fact that no one was more confused about the whole thing than me.

I gave her the all-patronizing slow clap.

"You got me, Erica. Well done. But if I'm honest, I'm shocked it took you this long."

"Well, when one hides so deep in the depths of South-A-fucking-Merica, it can become a real unending search."

I shook my head. "I wasn't hiding. I was waiting."

"Waiting for what?"

"C'mon, Erica. I think you know." When you don't know what to say, reassign the responsibility. The bluff would only work so long as I could continue to force information out of her. Information would keep me alive.

"I'm curious to know how thorough you've been," I said. "You tell me what you've got, and I'll tell you where you've gone wrong."

She folded her arms. "We understand your motive, Eighty-One. We know about Operation Shadow and the...flaws of the program."

I nodded. The flaws of Operation Shadow. A piece of the puzzle.

"Go on."

"It's a program that has been deleted from all records. It's why no one has seen your face. Until now."

"Go on."

"We know you had a reason for revenge and that you damn well took it."

I kept a stoic face. The intel was rolling in, and I didn't want to interrupt the flow.

"So far, so good."

"And then you disappear. Gone, like a ghost. Leaving us no trace. A wound to the ego of an agency that prides itself on hunting people down."

That was about as *CIA* as it gets. "Well, I'm sorry I hurt your feelings."

"Time went on, but you remained a mystery. Some thought you'd gotten yourself killed. Others thought you'd killed yourself. Officially, your file was permanently redacted. For a convenient while it was as if you had never existed. Until we began to hear murmurs of this...*El Flamingo.*"

You could tell she thought *El Flamingo* was a silly pseudonym, and I didn't appreciate it. The title had grown on me, to the point I now bore it with a sense of pride.

"We did some digging. We found that this *El Flamingo* was taking out undesirables all over the map: crew leaders, bosses, enforcers, corrupt cops, dirty politicians. Stealthy and lethal. Employing techniques unknown to most in his trade. Everyone thought he was some kind of a modern-day ninja. But not us. Very few agencies teach that kind of a skill set. No one wanted to admit it, but suspicion grew that maybe *El Flamingo* was someone known to us. That *El Flamingo* and Operative 81 were the same man."

"You're getting warmer."

"You were loyal to no one. You chose no side. And yet, you maintained some kind of moral code. Unlike most in your line of work, you were selective when accepting assignments. Fiercely so. If it involved children or families, you wouldn't touch it."

That made me feel better. Yes, I was playing a killer, but a principled killer. A likeable anti-hero, if you will.

"You left no trace of yourself, digital, or otherwise. For one to reach *El Flamingo*, it had to be old-school: payphones, letters, word-of-mouth. Quite unorthodox in this age of instant communication."

I shrugged. "Old school is untraceable."

Erica took a breath and recrossed her legs. "Tell me about Diego Flores."

"Well, he's the big fish, isn't he?"

"The biggest. Feared by all in the pond. Except for one person, Juan Moreno, the man who may well become the next president of Colombia. The final stone in Flores' way. We know it's the reason Flores has employed your services."

"Maybe he has. Maybe he hasn't."

"So here's the infamous *El Flamingo* in a position to capitalize on the biggest paycheck of his life, but what does he do? He calls on his sworn enemies, those who once betrayed him, those he vowed never to trust again. Why?"

If what she said was true, then *El Flamingo* had masterminded the whole thing. I pictured the situation from a bird's-eye-view, as if watching a piece of theatre slowly unravel. Among the cast there was the villainous crime boss, a rogue contract killer, a secretive American agency, and a wife whose loyalty was unknown.

Last but not least, we had the actor, sitting dumb in the middle of it all—and presently tied to a chair—the final piece to everyone's puzzle. Maybe if the situation wasn't so stressful, I would've seen the humor in it.

"Hello?" interrupted Erica. "Anyone home?"

"I'm just reflecting," I said. You'd think they would have learned by now that you don't rush a guy like *El Flamingo*.

I considered everything the real *El Flamingo* had

told me back on the Mexican coastline and paired it with what I heard now. He was an enigma, for sure, but while he had taken a turn down the violent path of, well, "typesetting," he seemed, at heart, like he was a good man. All that talk of love and second chances, and time passing by. Hell, the guy was a romantic! If you ask me, I believed that in his own wildly Flamingo-ish way, he'd been navigating a path toward the "right thing." I knew now just what to say to the increasingly impatient Erica.

"The things we do for love," I mused.

"What was that now?"

"It's about a woman."

"A woman?"

"A woman. But not just any woman."

"You'll have to elaborate."

"I'm in love."

Erica scratched her head. "That's…that's…new intel!"

"Well, tell the top floor at Langley you can't spy on the heart."

It sounded like a line from a shitty country song, but there you go.

"So you set this whole thing in motion for a woman?"

I remembered the way *El Flamingo* had spoken of the one he loved between sips of mezcal while peering into the dying sunset with eyes of regret, a rare glimpse into his lonely soul.

"Yes," I said. "A woman worth changing for."

Erica tucked her pen into her jacket. No games now.

"And saving Moreno? Why?"

"Someone once said that the greatest warrior is not the one who wins the war, but the one who prevents it."

"Get to the point."

"I've killed a lot of bad men in my life, but I've never saved a good one."

She hardened her gaze. Skeptical. I doubled down.

"This is what I've been waiting for. This is my chance to do some good in the world before I get too damned old. That's why I reached out. I can't do this alone. This is not a one-person job—not even for *El Flamingo*."

Erica leaned back in her chair and considered me for what felt like the same amount of time my head was in the bag. She twirled the pen in her hand, her focus renewed.

"One last thing I gotta know."

"Shoot." At this point, I was ready for anything.

"What kind of a contract killer names himself after a big, pink, harmless bird?"

I looked away and smiled into space. "The reasons are plentiful. Perhaps it's because Flamingos are patient, poised, and effortlessly stylish."

"You've got some kind of ego on you."

"Or, maybe it's something a little more layered," I continued. I was really in the zone now. "Maybe there is nothing more lethal than the perfect disguise. Like you say, a big, pink, harmless bird—what would be a better smokescreen for the most dangerous man in the world?"

Erica scoffed, but you could tell that, deep down, she was impressed.

She pushed back in her chair and stood up.

"What do we think?" she said. "Do we believe him?"

There it was again, the dreaded question. Was I believable?

All was quiet until someone behind me entered the room and broke the silence. "I believe him."

It was a voice I recognized, strong, smooth, husky, and the one of a woman in command.

I caught the delicious scent of perfume that had become wonderfully familiar—vanilla, roses, and another secret little ingredient. Everything slowed down, the way it does when your mind works out a million things in the space of a single moment.

Maria-Carla Flores stepped in front of me. I was suddenly aware of a truth that had been dangling under my nose all along.

Maria-Carla was a double agent!

But, by God, I stayed wholly in character. Without taking a beat, I gave her a knowing smile—as if I'd been expecting her the whole time.

"Maria-Carla, how was the bath?"

20

Hours later, Maria-Carla and I sat in subtle tension, catching the last rays of a westbound sun. We'd been let out of the safe house and dropped at a country club in the south of Cali. It was an open-plan barbeque *restaurante* with an expansive bar and large wooden tables.

We shared a traditional Colombian platter, the best kind of protein-laden meal a man can hope for post-interrogation: steak, grilled chicken, chorizo, *arroz*, *paprika-papas-fritas*, and about twenty different types of *empanada*.

Maria-Carla sipped from a can of *Poker cerveza*, eyeing me carefully. "There's still something you're not telling me," she said. "I wonder who you really are, underneath it all."

"I'm a man on his final mission."

If I told her the truth, would she ever believe it?

"You speak with such sincerity. Such confidence. But something is missing. Who were you before you were Operative 81? What is your real story?"

"I just got interrogated for the better part of an afternoon. I'm sick of my story. If it's all right with you, I'd like to know yours."

"I thought you already knew."

"I do. But I'd like to hear it from your lips."

She watched me chomp down the final empanada. "As you know, I work for the DNI," she said.

"The DNI. Right."

"The *Dirección Nacional de Inteligencia*."

"Of course."

"You must have heard of them."

"Of course I have," I said, trying to cover. "It's like the Colombian version of the CIA...right?"

"That is most certainly not our mission statement."

"Sorry. Please continue."

She peered reflectively into the rainforest on the distant horizon. "When I was younger, I was a singer."

I recalled Diego's story regarding the night he met her. He said he had never heard a voice so beautiful.

A flare of pain passed through Maria-Carla's eyes. "But something happened in my life. Something that changed what I wanted to be. So, I applied to the DNI."

She paused. "There, I was trained in espionage for a specific purpose: to become the perfect woman for Diego Flores. My mission was to create a weakness in a man who was considered unreachable. That was twenty-one years ago."

"And so they sent you in undercover. As a singer."

"Yes."

"So, this whole time you've been—"

"Living a lie."

"I was actually going to say playing a role." If you ask me, acting applies to everything.

"Things changed when I became pregnant. The lines got blurred. I never thought I would be raising the baby girl of a man I hated."

I handed her a napkin in case of any tears, but they didn't fall.

"Then this mission is the end for you too, right?"

"It's supposed to be. But something doesn't feel right."

"Meaning?"

"I can't stop thinking that Diego knows."

I recalled what Diego had told me at his desert driving range, *I no longer trust my wife.*

The waiter came over to clear the platter, pausing our conversation. Nearby birds chirped above the distant hum of central Cali, some miles away.

Once he was out of earshot, I asked, "Do you trust the CIA?"

"You can't trust anyone in this landscape, but there is no choice. The DNI was only able to implement the mission if we collaborated. At the time, the CIA was the only organization with knowledge of his location."

"I see."

I was able to piece certain elements together, but a lingering question remained. If Operative Eighty-One was a CIA agent gone rogue, and if he *had* disappeared for so long making a living off dark assignments under the alias of *El Flamingo*, to now find himself as the centerpiece of an international assassination, why disappear on the cusp of its conclusion? Why leave it all in the hands of a failed actor who happened to be at the right tiki-hut bar in Mexico at the just-right moment in time?

"We need to be careful tonight," said Maria-Carla.

I leaned in, serious. "Indeed we do."

"It's best we stay hidden. Camouflaged."

"My dear, I'm camouflage personified."

"In Cali, there is only one way to do that."

Not knowing what the hell she was getting at, I played along. "You know it. I know it. Everyone in Cali knows it."

"Exactly. So tell me. Do you dance salsa?"

A wave of panic set in. "Maria-Carla. I dance salsa like I roll out of bed."

Truth was, this flamingo had never danced salsa a day in its life. Goddamnit!

We took a ten-minute taxi ride toward the southern rainforest and were dropped at a small path that ascended the jungle hills.

We trekked for several minutes, and with the sun escaping, it was getting harder to see. I began to feel like I was about to be whacked.

"You're telling me there's a salsa bar out here? We're in the middle of a damn jungle."

She smiled, a light sheen of sweat glowing on her forehead.

"You're in Cali. There is a salsa bar *everywhere*. You just need to know where to look."

El Flamingo had said the same thing about aces.

We arrived at a steep bend that looked out onto a single set of lights in the distance, when I finally heard a surreal echo from the depths of the valley trees—a singing voice accompanied by a piano and the pipe of a trumpet.

Maria-Carla stopped to listen, then smiled.

"*¿Me crees ahora?*"

Do you believe me now?

"*Si. Te creo.*"

We followed the music and lights as the beat of the salsa grew louder, until, through the trees we sighted the shapes of dancing shadows, stepping in perfect time, a scene choreographed by culture.

At last, we came to the small brick salsa house where a multitude of colors decorated the walls, like the wings of a rare parrot.

At the door, a curly-haired woman in a bright yellow dress greeted us with a kiss on the cheek and a bright grin, as if we were all in on a secret. Then, she opened the door to the fiesta.

There was a smoke glaze to the atmosphere lit by soft candle lamps; dark enough to cast shadows, but bright enough to illuminate smiles. The crowd was a soul in motion, dancing in close quarters, leaving just enough room for us to weave through, making our way to the bar.

In the middle of it all, a pianist and a trumpeter stood on either side of an old man who sang into a microphone, lyrics that spoke of happiness amidst constant pain. His eyes were sheltered by the downward tilt of his Panama hat, but a savvy smile escaped from under the rim.

At the bar, Maria-Carla ordered for us.

"*Dos Aguardientes,*" she said.

"Arguar-what?" I asked her.

"*Aguardientes*. Firewater!"

The bartender placed a couple of shot glasses in front of us. With the flip of a bottle and the twist of a cap, he filled both with a single pour, one to the other. We said *salud*, clinked glasses, and threw them back. The shot was strong, sweet and it scorched the hell out of my throat. Maria-Carla leaned in and said, "It's time to salsa."

I froze in place, the fear of God clasping my heart. The thought of dancing scared me more than the damn assassination.

"One moment," I said.

I turned back to the bartender and held out my empty shot glass. He laughed and poured me another. There was no way in hell I would attempt this sober.

We merged into the dance floor, barely fitting into the crowd.

"Are you sure there's room for us?"

"Of course there is," she said. "Why do you think salsa steps are so small? It's meant to be danced in a crowded place."

Maria-Carla peered into my eyes expectantly. "Now. Are you going to lead, or am I?"

Think, Galloway! I'd once seen a sitcom where the main loveable idiot takes a salsa class. What was it? Left foot forward, right foot back? Step left, middle, step right? Do I step first, or did she? If in doubt, spin? No! Don't spin, for Christ's sake. Someone could get seriously hurt.

I stood out like a horse in a yoga class, and there was no hiding it. The beautiful portrait of a dancing ensemble, smeared by the big *gringo* blotch right in the middle. Maria-Carla laughed and moved a little closer.

"So then, Flamingo, is there anything you want to tell me?"

Her hips moved daringly close to mine, as thinking straight became an increasingly taller task.

"I lied about the salsa."

"You certainly did."

"I'm sorry. I just didn't want you to think of me as uncultured."

She leaned closer and commanded me to relax and follow her lead. "Listen to the count. *Uno, dos, tres*, middle, *cuatro, cinco, seiz*, middle."

Our fingers intertwined, she stepped to the right, then back to the middle, pulling me with her.

"Now, move your hips. Feel the music. Feel my body."

Easy, Lou. Think of baseball.

Whatever the hell that "firewater" was, its magic was taking effect. I no longer felt like the worst dancer in the world. I was swaying and sliding, swooping and gliding, listing forward and back, the rhythm more powerful than my own embarrassment. Before long, I'd fooled myself into thinking I had the salsa down, all credit to Maria-Carla.

The band faded out of one song into another, a little slower this time. Same steps, same count, but we could take our time.

Maria-Carla's eyes turned resolute. She spun me out again. I seemed to have no control over which way I went. She spun me back in.

"The salsa wasn't the only thing you lied about, was it?"

"I have no idea what you're referring to."

"It's time to tell the truth."

She whipped me back out, keeping hold of my wrist, sending me twirling so close to the bar I nearly wiped out a row of women. Maria-Carla reeled me back in.

"You know the truth," I said, trying to catch my breath.

"No. I don't."

She forced herself against me, wrapping her hand around the back of my neck, her smile disappearing. "Who are you really?"

Between the steps and the spins and the twists and
the turns, I was stripped of all focus. *This* was the real
interrogation. And she was good, good enough to have
me slipping out of character. I fought with everything
I had. With an arm around her lower back, I pulled her
close to try to assert some kind of control. *El Flamingo*:
when he's on the dance floor, he means business.

"I'm *El Flamingo!*"

She spun me again. "No! You're no killer. I knew
that the moment I saw you."

She pulled me back again, ferociously. "I saw something in you. Something I had not seen in a long time."

A sucker for her charms, I had to know. "What did
you see?"

"The soul of a good man."

With the music building to a crescendo, it seemed all
eyes were on us. Maria-Carla spun me around a final
time and then came so close to my face our lips almost
touched.

"Who are you?"

At that moment, I broke character. I'd lost the battle. I wanted her to know who I was. In fact, I wanted
to tell her everything.

"It wasn't a fake," I said.

"What?"

"The driver's license. It was real. That was me."

She pulled me closer.

"So—?"

"My name is Lou Galloway, and I'm just an actor."

"An actor?"

"A failed actor. And I don't know what the hell to do
next or how the hell I got here. But I'm glad I did."

She took a moment to absorb the truth, a truth so
unpredictable it couldn't possibly have been imagined.
Then her eyes softened, and she let out a slow exhala-
tion like a burden had finally been lifted.

"*Gracias*, Lou Galloway."

Her lips were just an inch away. Everything about the moment said to kiss her. She finally saw me for who I was. Who I *really* was. That right there is one hell of a thing.

I tilted my head. She did the same. She closed her eyes. I closed mine.

Here it was, coming in hot, a fiery arrow from a bullseye Cupid; a kiss from the woman of my wildest dreams....

But, before our lips could touch, the room exploded with applause, breaking the intimacy, leaving us no choice but to pull away.

We stepped back and faced the crowd of passionate revelers who had become our audience. The bartender raised a glass. The old vocalist tipped his hat. In return, I simply winked and smiled, as if my salsa abilities were a gift from God.

There was a feeling in the air that tomorrow might never come, and that would be okay. Nothing mattered except the here-and-now of this jungle-concealed salsa bar.

As the excitement subsided, I realized I was deep into one of the great moments of my life, the ones you remember when you're near the end of it all. We hadn't kissed, but the two of us were about to. Sometimes, that's as good as it gets. Happiness is fleeting, but it's in those fleeting moments that we become our best selves.

Then something caught my eye, disturbing my romanticism.

A shadow in the back corner of the bar—still, and alone—was out of place enough to catch my attention. The shadow turned his back, downed his drink, and headed for the door. I never caught a glimpse of his face. Someone had been watching. Someone who didn't want to be seen.

21

Soon after midnight, Maria-Carla and I stepped out of the smoky heat of the fiesta and into the jungle breeze. I think we both knew that some things are meant to be lived only once; that we'd never return to that secret little salsa bar.

We made our way back down the moonlit pathway as sprinkling raindrops fell from the leaves and kissed our skin. We reached the main road, taxied back to the city, and hopped out at Parque San Antonio, which overlooks the lights of the urban valley.

The locals were out and about. Couples, teenagers, and families had all gathered as one to take in the sights. There's no such thing as a late night in Colombia.

Maria-Carla looked away from the view and fixed her eyes on me. "I need to know how this all began."

"Where do I start?"

"With the truth."

So, I told her everything. From before Arturo emerged out of the Mexican street shadows. Before I met *El Flamingo* and put on his feathered fedora. Before the mezcal and the worm that lay at the bottom. I began with Los Angeles.

"I went to L.A. thinking I would become the greatest actor ever known. I had this idea that acting was a superpower, and if I used it the right way, maybe I could do something important. If I worked hard, focused on craft, on character, on storytelling, I thought one day I would put something of value into the world."

Lou Galloway: noble thespian, spilling his vulnerable soul to a Colombian intelligence agent. Who would have thought.

"But time went by. Money ran out. I landed one or two meaningless roles here and there. Soap operas. Commercials. Nothing of any real substance. Next thing you know, I'm thirty-five years old with nothing to show for my dream-chasing. In the blink of an eye, I had nothing to lose. That's when I said, 'To hell with it.'"

"Then you went to Mexico?"

"And ended up at the same bar as *El Flamingo.*"

"So, what did the two of you talk about?"

"It was a real country-song exchange."

"What does that mean?"

"It means we had the kind of conversation that only happens in country songs, where you shoot the shit, speak in broad terms, and muse over life's mysteries."

"Such as?"

"Choices. Love. How to play an ace when you don't have one. Where we've been, where we're going, and where we could have gone."

"A country-song exchange," she repeated. "You're a very strange man, Lou Galloway."

I had the feeling she was flirting with me.

"It sounds like you and *El Flamingo* shared a bond."

"You could say that. I guess we were two guys looking for a way out of where we were."

"We're all looking for a way out," she said. "I had been trapped on this mission for too long. I couldn't take it anymore. I had a plan to escape, to take my daughter and run. I was ready. But then, from nowhere, he reached out."

Maria-Carla shifted closer. "A hand-written letter appeared in a DNI safe house addressed to me, signed *El Flamingo.* He knew I was undercover. It was a warning."

I saw what Erica meant by "old-school."

"He told me his story, detailing the events of Operation Shadow, from a time he was referred to as 'Operative Eighty-One.' He was working deep cover, infiltrating the chain of command between Colombia and Mexico. Then, suddenly, he was sold out."

In terms of character backstory, this was an actor's goldmine. I hung on the rhythm of her words as her hair danced with the midnight breeze.

"I think of corruption like a cancer. While it starts small, it spreads until nothing is untouched. Drug money found its way into the program, and Eighty-One's cover was blown."

Maria-Carla pushed her hair out of her eyes.

"He was left to a certain death, but they underestimated him. Not only did he survive, he returned to haunt them. One by one, he hunted down those who set him up. Everyone who ever knew his true identity was killed. Then, he disappeared."

She told the story with cinematic fire in her voice. I imagined notes from a Latin guitar over grainy, flickering film, playing out in a box office adaptation that would never be made, because it would never be known.

"Years later, when a *sicario* emerged under the pseudonym of *El Flamingo*, the CIA suspected Eighty-One. There are very few on the planet with his level of expertise. His track record showed he could eliminate just about anyone, undetected, like he was never there at all. Many of his targets had been considered untouchable. Quite simply, he is the best in the world."

"Which is why Diego hired him," I said.

"Yes. But Diego made a mistake. He never suspected *El Flamingo* to have a moral code. After he initiated contact with the DNI, there was only one missing link."

"Juan Moreno."

"And, lucky for us, Juan Moreno is a brave man."

"So, the idea was to sting Diego in the midst of his very own assassination attempt on Moreno?"

"Yes, but *El Flamingo* had anticipated there would be a leak. He has never trusted the CIA. Not after what they did to him. It's why he told me to obtain some kind of insurance."

"Insurance?"

"The prayer beads I gave you. Are they still safe?"

I'd forgotten all about them. I took the beads from my pocket and handed them to her. She twisted the little cross into two separate pieces, and a small electronic chip fell into her palm.

"On this chip is a map that leads to a file that contains all the information I was able to obtain on Diego. It holds the names of business associates and employees involved in his operation: from Colombia, through Mexico, and into the United States."

"And you wouldn't trust the CIA with this?"

"No."

"But you trusted *El Flamingo.*"

She nodded.

"Why?"

"Because if he wanted to sell me out, he would have already done it."

She returned the microchip inside the cross, clicked it back together, and handed it back to me.

"If all else fails, this is all we have."

I noticed she had clenched a fist, suppressing a rage beneath the surface. I put my hand on hers. "Hey. The fight's not over, Maria-Carla. Not if *El Flamingo* has anything to say about it."

"And by that, do you mean him, or you?"

"Frankly, my dear, I'm really not sure anymore."

We let the moment last as long as we could. Around us, the locals were beginning to disperse and head home. Before we did the same, there was one more thing I just had to ask. "How did he get the name *El Flamingo?*"

Maria-Carla stared toward the skyline. "There are many theories. The story I heard goes that on a night in a Mexican resort town, a *jefe* on vacation had taken a woman to his hotel room. She was drugged and forced against her will. She remembered dancing

with friends, then feeling suddenly weak. She was
pulled away to a hotel room. The whole night was a
blur, but there was one thing she was sure of. When
she woke, the man who took her lay dead on the floor.
Suffocated, according to the police report. She had
been left unharmed and was able to catch a glimpse of
someone else, a stranger, leaving the room. When the
police asked for a description of the stranger, she said,
'*Nunca le vi la cara. Pero llevaba una camisa rosa. Fue
como si un flamenco me hubiera salvado.*'"

Maria-Carla let me decipher the Spanish for myself.

"She said that she did not see his face, but that he
wore a pink shirt."

"Correct. Your Spanish is improving, Lou."

Your tomorrows may not be guaranteed, but there's
always time for a little Spanish lesson.

"And what was the last thing she said?"

I couldn't help but smile.

"She said that it was like she was saved by a
flamingo."

22

The doors of La Vela de Cali parted as the concierge greeted us with a smile that shone like the gel in his hair. The pianist still tinkled away in the corner of the hotel bar. It appeared that he never left his piano, no matter the hour. Whether or not he was indeed a spy, you couldn't question his work ethic.

"Let's see the rooftop," said Maria-Carla.

Maybe she didn't want the night to end just yet, either.

The elevator ride was a new kind of tense. We had traded our secrets and unleashed our souls. We'd covered corruption, espionage, and plots of vengeance. But this particular here-and-now was a new mood. This was late-night rom-com, complete with first-kiss-looming butterflies. We stepped onto the rooftop. Across the valley there shined the scattered lights of the *comuna* houses, like a gathering of a thousand fireflies.

"*¿Un último baile?*" asked Maria-Carla.

One last dance?

Naturally, I obliged. Taking her by the hand, we moved in unison, nice and slow, our only music the faraway rhythms rising from the downtown salsa bars. I held her soft and close as she whispered in my ear.

"Out of all the failed actors in the world, *El Flamingo* sure chose well."

A sweet, small, and gingerly delivered backhand compliment. I asked her to elaborate.

"Well," she said, "*El Flamingo* seems to be one step ahead of everyone. I think he chose you for a reason. You were a piece to the puzzle. He needed someone to adopt his identity. Who could portray the many layers to his character? It had to be a complete unknown, but also a man with the talent to pull it off."

"Thank God I never made it in Hollywood," I said. "Or you and I might never have met."

Shit. Had I said that out loud?

"I mean...or else this whole mission would've been a real shit-show," I stuttered, trying to get the cat back in the damn bag.

I thought I might've glimpsed the slightest smile from Maria-Carla, but I couldn't be sure. We stayed a while longer; left-foot-middle, right-foot-back, until I gave her a final twirl.

"It's getting cold," she said.

"I guess we better call it a night."

We admired the city lights one last time. *Buenas noches, Cali.*

We stepped back in the elevator and hit the button for our floor.

She glanced my way.

I glanced back.

We both glanced at the floor. Don't forget to breathe, Lou, ya nervous bastard.

The elevator doors parted. We edged down the vintage corridor, guided by the glimmer of antique bulbs. I scanned us into the suite. Maria-Carla slipped off her shoes, then walked over to the floor-to-ceiling window. She stood silhouetted by the night sky, and the dim shadows gave the suite the glow of a deserted theatre set.

In those same shadows glinted something else. The goddamn wedding band around her finger.

She's not really married, Lou. She's undercover.

Diego was an evil man. I had no respect for who he was or what he stood for, but I had a strange respect for that ring.

But then again, there she was, watching and waiting, etched in starlight, deep into the midnight hour. What is it about a lone beauty gazing into the night?

I channelled my best Cary Grant. "A fine evening, madam, wasn't it?"

She responded only with her eyes, which I saw in

the faint reflection of the window. They weren't admiring the city view any longer. They were locked on me. I told myself not to mind the ring. The marriage wasn't real. Just stroll on over there and kiss her lips.

"*El Flamingo* is master of his craft," she said. "But so are you, Lou. I can see that. You're a brilliant actor."

"I focus on the craft of character work and hope for the best," I said, stammering away like I'd never spoken to a woman before.

Time was ticking. This could be the greatest night of your life, or your biggest regret. Get a goddamn move on, Lou.

She waited still, giving me every last ounce of the chance at hand.

You're losing it, Lou. Take the risk. Take the goddamn risk!

My heart pounded as she waited for one final moment.

Christ's sake Lou, we could all die tomorrow!

Then she waited no more. She turned away and said, "Get some sleep, Lou."

And there it is. You let it slip.

I thanked her for the dance. She said *de nada*. I walked to my empty room and shut the door.

Lou, you're a goddamned coward.

23

It was a hellish night's sleep, dipping in and out of a restless doze, neither asleep nor awake.

Who the hell was *El Flamingo*? As an actor, you're supposed to be as acquainted with your character as you are with your own self. With regard to this character, I still had a lot to learn.

El Flamingo was an enigma. His name unknown. His face unseen. His intentions unclear. As Operative 81, he had flipped the script on the CIA, leaving them scratching their heads, bewildered by their own brand of darkness.

But who was he really? On a deeper level. What made him tick? What went on inside his mind? Who did he see when he looked in the mirror? What was his inner monologue? How did he perceive himself? Most importantly, what did he want?

El Flamingo's words on the Mexican beach echoed over and over, in no particular order, a nonsensical ramble taken from a conversation I'd thought meant nothing at all—but now, I knew, held all the answers.

You ever been in love?

What is it?—a gamble or an investment?

I might just have something for you.

Watch my hat.

I relived the lost moment with Maria-Carla and cursed myself again. Maybe, in a parallel universe, it would have played out differently. I wouldn't have frozen. I wouldn't have left her waiting. I would have gone to her and kissed her; gentle, slow, and patient, because when you have the night, you have forever.

I pictured her soft linen dress falling to the floor. I imagined her naked body wrapped around me in the silk sheets of the canopy bed. You could say it was a dose of pleasant imagery. Hell, you could say it was just about heaven.

A startling succession of loud knocks woke me from my dream. I sat up fast to see Arturo, his eyes alight with urgency having burst through my door.

"Flamingo. Listen to me. You need to evacuate right now."

"Why? What's happening?"

"People are coming for you. They are making an attempt. Take Maria-Carla and get out."

"Who is coming for me?"

"There's no time. Just take Maria-Carla and go!"

He turned to rush out. "Arturo," I yelled. "Where are you going?"

He looked back at me like a war hero about to save the whole platoon. "To create a diversion."

He darted from the room and disappeared.

Shocked and confused, I hurled on my jeans and the nearest shirt, then hurried through the attaching door into Maria-Carla's quarters. She was already a step ahead of me, fully dressed, loading a black handgun.

"Arturo said—"

"I know," she said, her voice firm but unpanicked. "Go get your gun."

Yes, ma'am.

I rummaged through the bag, found the gun, and strapped on the holster. Maria-Carla opened the hallway door, checked both directions, and led us down the corridor toward the elevator.

After thirty long seconds, it arrived, full of unsuspecting guests.

One of them was a tall man with combed hair and hollow eyes. Both his hands were tucked into the pockets of a black leather jacket.

The guests shifted aside—all except the tall man, who remained still. Everyone moves a little when someone new enters an elevator. It's human nature. They step to the side or clear their throat, or glance at their phone. Not this guy. He was expecting us.

Maria-Carla looked my way. She'd made him, too. The button was lit for level eight where the gym and pool were located. Maria-Carla gave me a look that said, "stay cool and don't do anything stupid." While I would try to obey, I couldn't make any promises.

At the eighth floor, we all stepped out, but just before the doors closed, Maria-Carla checked her phone, paused, and abruptly turned back as if she'd forgotten something. Out of nowhere, she kneed the tall man square in the nuts, following with a gut punch and a chop to the neck. He dropped to the ground as a pair of pistols tumbled from his jacket pockets.

"Jesus," I said.

Maria-Carla turned to the trembling guests. *"Todos ustedes deben irse,"* she said. *"Ahora!"*

You all need to leave. Now!

Nobody questions a woman who's just permanently disabled an armed man before their eyes.

"Let them go first," she said. "It's us they want."

They all hustled back into the elevator, murmuring to each other in collective shock. We watched the elevator doors close, and the numbers travel to the ground floor. Almost immediately, it started back up. Maria-Carla shook her head.

"More are coming. Let's take the stairs."

She drew her sidearm with flair. If there was a magazine called *The Espionage Weekly*, she'd be the cover girl. We ran down the hall toward the stairway door. Her eyes were focused. Her voice was low.

"Stay close behind me."

We entered the stairwell. Maria-Carla made short, sharp checks; left to right, up and down.

Clear.

We quickly descended the winding stairs.

A couple of flights down, a stairwell door popped open. A man in a black ski mask jumped in, armed with a semi-automatic.

He aimed our way, but Maria-Carla fired three quick rounds before he could get off a shot. Three hits, right in the torso. The masked figure clutched his stomach, let out a yelp, and dropped to his knees.

I was shaking, but Maria-Carla was as cool as a Colombian *cholado*. Farther below, a team of masked assailants ascended the stairs. Shouts were exchanged as they zeroed in on us. They fired up the middle of the stairway. We jumped backward as bullets ricocheted off the walls.

I tried to stay calm and in character. You're *El Flamingo*, a man poised in chaos, who will dance with the Devil 'til the dame gets dizzy, who, in a hail of bullets hears nothing but smooth jazz, who—

"Snap out of it!" screamed Maria-Carla through a cloud of gun smoke. "Are you hit?"

I quickly patted myself down. "If I am, I've gone into shock and blocked out the pain."

"You're fine. Now get up."

We bolted back up the stairs to level eight, entered through the fire exit, and sprinted down the hallway. We took cover in the corner, opposite two separate doors. One read *Piscina*—Spanish for pool. The other said *Gimnasio*—Spanish for gymnasium.

"Get out your gun," said Maria-Carla.

I drew the Smith & Wesson from its holster and handed it to her. She pulled a handful of bullets from a strap on her inner thigh, loaded the gun, and handed it back. Definitely a multi-page spread for *The Espionage Weekly*. She showed me the switch on the side of her own weapon in a quickfire demonstration.

She flicked up the switch. "Safety on."

She flicked it down. "Safety off. Got it?"

I flicked it up. "Got it."

Lou Galloway: Recently certified in *How to Use a Gun in Ten Seconds*.

Down the hall, the stairwell door clanged open, followed by scuttling footsteps. I mirrored her technique, our backs tight against the wall, our guns pointing upward.

A pair of dark shapes fired as they dashed across the hallway gap. Maria-Carla fired back, buying us time. My ears were ringing like crazy, but I could make out the click of reloading guns.

"There were two of them," she said. "We need to split them up."

Maria-Carla nodded toward the gym door. "Get inside there, and I'll cover you. Wait there and be ready to shoot. Can you handle that?"

I hesitated.

"When you say 'shoot,' you mean actually *at* the guy?"

"You're a genius."

She stepped back to aim. Knowing the bullets were about to fly right past my head, I hoped to holy hell that she was a strong markswoman.

She held up three fingers.

Then two.

Then one.

I flew across the gap and dove through the door, narrowly dodging the zinging of gunfire. Perhaps I was just too stupid to die? I slammed the door shut, then bobbed up to look through the small window.

Maria-Carla gave me a thumbs up. We were okay.

I reached for my gun, but it wasn't there. I peeked out the window again and saw it lying in the middle of the hallway.

Shit!

Maria-Carla held up a palm. Stay back!

I backed up, looked around, and realized the benefit of where I was—a freakin' gym! I didn't have a gun, but there were barbells, dumbbells, and kettlebells. Hell, there was even a battle rope. To *El Flamingo*, any object is a potential weapon.

I loaded a bar with forty-five pounders on each side and rolled it to the door. A giant tripwire. Then I picked up a couple of dumbbells that were light enough to throw, but heavy enough to hurt. I faced the door, crouched low, and waited.

Any second now.

The door flew open. A masked assailant charged through, shooting up the room with a spray of bullets, but the blast went astray as he stumbled over the bar and lost his gun. He hauled himself to his feet, but not before I lobbed three dumbbells at him in rapid succession.

The first one missed. Wide left.

The second was straight on but a couple of inches too high as he ducked down into a deep squat.

On his way up, the third one hit him. Right in the groin, jeopardizing any of his future plans for procreation. The assailant gasped in agony and dropped to his knees.

In just moments, he gathered himself, stood up, and drew a long machete strapped to his belt, even managing a voracious smirk.

In turn, I picked up a twenty-pound kettlebell.

I'd done a little stage combat in my time. I figured this was no different. (Except the blood wouldn't be ketchup and actual death was a possibility.) The guy tried a swipe at me, but I stepped aside. He poked the machete toward my chest, but I batted it away. I swung the kettlebell for his head, but he countered with a left punch. My mouth filled with the taste of blood, but I spat it out like it was nothin'. Bruce Willis. *Die Hard*. Act Three.

He lunged at my face with the machete, like he wanted to stab me in the damn eye. But years of kettlebell swings had trained my instincts. As an actor, you need to stay in shape. I managed to bob underneath the blade, which carried me into a squat. Then I used all the power from my thighs, glutes, and core to explode upward, catching him right on the chin. I felt the weight crack into his jaw.

He was out cold and flat on his back. I carefully made my way into the corridor, retrieved my gun, and headed for the door that said *piscina*. Inside it was humid and thick with the scent of chlorine.

A body floated in the middle of the pool in a spreading cloud of red.

Thank God, it wasn't Maria-Carla.

"*¿Todo bien?*" I turned to see her reloading her Magnum.

"*Todo bien,*" I confirmed. "I broke my guy's jaw with a kettlebell."

"Good work. Now let's move."

We made a break for the elevator.

"Up or down?" I asked.

"Up."

"Up? As in the roof?"

"Yes."

"How is that logical?"

"Downstairs is surrounded! We need a different way. The roof is our only choice."

Goddamnit! Rooftop it would have to be.

I hit the button about ten times in a row like a junior Wall Street broker late for his first face-to-face with the CEO. The light was on for level twenty-three, and we were on the eighth. The elevator moved to twenty, then eighteen, taking its sweet old time.

Hurry the hell up.

We heard the stairway door open. Another one coming.

Sixteen.

Fourteen.

The footsteps were closing in.

Twelve.

Ten.

Finally, the doors opened. Maria-Carla shoved me in and held down the "close" button, but a gloved hand snaked in and forced the doors back open. Another ski-masked bastard! He put the gun to my head. So, this was how it would end? Shot between the eyes, halfway through the greatest acting performance of all time?

Maybe not. Maria-Carla had her gun to the assailant's temple. Stalemate.

His eyes flicked to Maria-Carla's, then back to mine. I watched his finger on the trigger.

I closed my eyes and braced myself for the end.

Instead, I heard a yelp of pain.

Was that me?

I opened my eyes just before the elevator doors closed. The assailant was flat on the ground, pinned underneath the wheels of a tall luggage trolley controlled by none other than a courageous bell boy. I tried to see his face, but his back was turned, and the elevator doors shut before I ever got the chance.

24

"That there was the best bellboy in the world!" I yelled.

At the rooftop, we stepped out into the sharp morning light, where only a few hours before, we'd danced under the moon. This morning, we were fleeing armed men who'd appeared out of nowhere, hellbent on killing us. What a difference a day makes.

Our next move would come down to two options: one on the right; one on the left.

To our right was an even higher building, separated by about a fifty-foot gap. Impossible.

To our left was another hotel, just a couple of floors shorter than *La Vela de Cali*. On its roof was an infinity pool. I glanced at Maria-Carla, who appeared to be calculating our possibilities. It was about a forty-foot leap into a fair-sized rectangular pool—still plenty of room for error—not impossible, but pretty damn close. If this gorgeous madwoman suggested we jump, I would flat out refuse.

We moved to the building's edge nonetheless. I looked down. A wave of vertigo made me dizzy.

Below was an army of cars marked *Policia*, their sirens wailing. Officers surrounded the building, their guns drawn, shouting commands. In another place in the world this would be a welcome sight, but here in Cali, you couldn't know. The police could be working for anyone. We couldn't risk being taken into custody. Who knows where we would end up.

Maria-Carla spoke in a voice with the calm of a leisurely stroll.

"Listen. We need to jump."

I looked from the building edge to her, then back again. A swirl of fear gripped my stomach.

"No."

"Yes."

"No."

128

"We have to."

"I will not!"

"You shall!"

Maria-Carla took my hand, appearing to have decided for me, but I tugged away. I wasn't going to have it.

Then the stairwell door opened. Another masked assailant stepped out. Maria-Carla fired a round that forced him to momentarily retreat behind the stairway door.

"*Vamos!*" she yelled.

Grabbing my wrist, she exploded off the mark, pulling me with her. I had no choice. We galloped toward the building's edge like a pair of sprinters in sight of the finish line.

Gunshots went off behind us.

We ran out of roof.

Then we had lift-off, our momentum soaring upward and out. We flew through the air. Time pressed pause. We were no longer sprinters, but momentary eagles. The infinity pool looked suddenly smaller, like the bullseye on a dartboard after one tequila too many.

I focused solely on gliding toward the blue, pedalling through the air, not letting go of Maria-Carla's hand. I was sure I was screaming, but I heard only silence.

My eardrums exploded as I was sucked into a rushing cold. Water flooded my eyes, nose, and mouth, and my heart hadn't beaten since take-off.

Maria-Carla's hand was still clutched in mine. We were still together. Christ on a bike, we'd made it.

With no air in my lungs, I kicked upward toward the light until we finally broke the surface and gasped for air.

Any celebration for having successfully made the jump was quickly halted by the spray of incoming gunfire. Bullets made a hundred tiny splashes around us. Hotel guests screamed and scattered. We managed to swim to the closest corner of the pool and took cover, keeping our heads out of the firing line.

I realized I'd dropped the Smith & Wesson yet again. This time it must've fallen thirty floors down, quite possibly hitting an escaping guest. Guns kill.

By some kind of miracle, Maria-Carla still had her Glock. She brought it up from the water, cocked it, and shook it off.

"That thing waterproof?"

"Let's find out."

She pointed it upward and faced me.

"He will need to reload soon. When he does, we take him out. To get a clear shot, I need elevation. I need to sit on your shoulders."

"Sorry?"

"I need to wrap my legs around your shoulders!"

I gave her a heroic smoulder. "I'm the man for the job."

The shooting came in five-second bursts, followed by a four-second pause.

We counted it out. One, two, three, four, five.

"Get ready," she said.

I took a breath, bobbed under water, and swam up between her legs. Her toned thighs wrapped around my neck like the world's most arousing travel pillow. If not for the gunfire, this would have been incredible.

She locked her ankles around me. I put both of my hands around her firm glutes, purely to secure her, of course. *El Flamingo*: count on him to put safety first.

I prepared for take-off.

One, two, three, four, five!

Maria-Carla squeezed my neck.

It was go-time.

I dipped down to feel my feet on the pool floor, and with all the power I could muster, I sprang up, hoping to give her enough lift for a clear shot.

For a split second, I looked the killer in the eye, his blood-thirsty glare meeting my own.

Then his head jerked back in a spray of pink mist, timed exactly with the blast of Maria-Carla's gun. I was the last thing he ever saw. *Adios, parcero.*

G'bye, partner.

We plunged back underwater. I slid out from between Maria-Carla's thighs, with the hope to someday return.

We fought our way out of the pool against the weight of our soaked clothes and ran to the poolside cabana. We quickly donned a couple of abandoned bathrobes from the laundry cart.

Maria-Carla retrieved her wallet from her dress and tucked it into her robe along with her weapon.

There we were, back on the move, perfectly camouflaged by the robes, just another couple of hotel patrons, scared shitless and running for our lives. We hurried through the lobby and broke onto the street.

Tires screeched as more cop cars surrounded the building.

Maria-Carla took my hand.

"This way."

We headed toward the main road that eventually connected to the highway. Now the robes looked ridiculous. Extra attention was the last thing we needed. After we'd put a block between the hotel and us, Maria-Carla hailed the first taxi we saw.

The driver was a chubby man with wild eyebrows and wheezy breath. We slid into the back. Maria-Carla gave him a firm command in rapid-fire Spanish..

You need to drive us out of the city to the mountains, as fast as possible. And don't give us any bullshit!

His smile dropped and his eyes bulged. He gulped once and faced the front like he was in the starting blocks of the Indy 500, before accelerating, pedal-to-the-metal, heading in the direction of the southwest jungle. Sure enough, he gave us no bullshit.

I asked Maria-Carla where we were going.

"The only place I know we will be safe."

25

The engine of the beaten-down taxi strained against the incline of the valley roads, barely making it out of second gear. The driver glanced nervously in the rear-view mirror, embarrassed at the rusty howl of his ride, desperate not to fail the terrifying beauty behind him.

In silence, we gazed out at the endless row of palm trees that bordered the highway, as rays of midday *sol* sliced through the leaves.

I was still in a mild state of shock, but the surge in adrenaline was wearing off, replaced by the pressing questions in my mind, ringing like the echoes of gunfire.

"Do you think Arturo escaped?"

"I don't know," said Maria-Carla.

"The men who came for us. Who sent them?"

She was silent for a while. "They didn't come for us. They came for you."

I thought back and realized they had specifically targeted me, *"El Flamingo,"* as opposed to Maria-Carla. "I guess you could say they were trying to '*assassinate my character,*'" I offered. While this was no time for jokes, I felt it too good to hold inside.

"This is no time for jokes," she confirmed.

"I agree. I just thought a dash of comic relief could help keep us calm."

"You thought wrong."

"You're right. It was brilliant, but poorly timed. I apologize."

"Quiet!" she ordered.

"Arturo knew they were coming before we did."

"And he warned us. If it wasn't for him, we'd be dead."

"But how did he know? Whoever he is, he is not who he says."

I tried to keep a calm voice, free of panic, like we were solving a crossword on a Sunday morning.

"Who else had knowledge of our location?"

"Someone who works for Diego," she said. "Or Diego himself. That's why you were the target. If he wanted me dead, he would kill me himself."

"Is he really capable of that?"

She looked me dead in the eye. "He's capable of anything."

"All those years ago, Operation Shadow was corrupted by drug money," I started. Lou Galloway: intercontinental mystery solver, deduces the facts. "What if it has happened again? A mole within the CIA?"

"It's possible. It's what *El Flamingo* suspected."

If *El Flamingo* was right, it would have destroyed all she'd worked for, the same way it had for him those years before. We needed to simplify what we already knew and focus on the bright spots.

"Someone is on our side," I said. "It's the only way Arturo could have known."

"Either way, it's compromised."

"Sure. It's compromised. But still..."

"Still...what?"

"We stay the course. If we don't, Juan Moreno dies."

She remained in thought for a while, then met my eyes. "You could run away. There is still time."

"Stop right there."

"No one knows who you are. You could still escape."

"I won't hear another word."

"This was never your fight."

"This was *always* my fight. I've never done anything that mattered. I'd been heading for this my whole life. I'm not running either, Maria-Carla. Not until we finish this damn thing."

She studied me closely. "The odds are against us."

Ever the actor, I replied, "That's the only way I've ever known them."

If things went pear-shaped in the next twenty-four hours, we'd be goners. But hell, if I died at her side, would that be so bad?

I recalled *El Flamingo*'s words from back at the tiki bar. "Someone once told me that you don't have to *have* an ace to *play* an ace."

"And who was that someone?"

I shrugged. "Some guy who sells typesetting, but I think it applies here."

It evoked from her a momentary smile. "So you're still in?"

"I was in from—"

The moment I first saw you.

I bit my tongue before I actually said the words, thinking the sentence was better left unfinished. It felt like a line from a B-grade romance, and we weren't quite ready for that. At least not yet.

"I'm all in."

She observed me for a spell. Impassive.

"Lou Galloway," she said, almost to herself. "What a man."

"I know," I said. "Some might even say...a hero."

At that, she rolled her eyes, then without warning, scooched over and planted a kiss on my cheek. It lasted only a split second before she turned away.

"I'm sorry, I didn't quite catch that. Could you repeat the kiss?"

"*Silencio*," she said.

And so, once again, I thought that this must be a fictional universe. An outlandish tale penned by some punk of an author whose mind had all but gone west.

However it had come to pass, I was happy to be here.

We were on the run, with everything to lose and the fight of our lives ahead. Some would say there's no better feeling.

Dark clouds hovered over the jungle ahead, the sign of a storm rolling in. The horizon seemed eternal, the kind that leads to the unknown, reaching out for the ends of the earth, reminding you how small you are, and that if you ran forever, you'd never get anywhere.

26

The taxi followed the curves of a rural highway, a forest maze where brightly colored birds soared and coffee beans grew. We passed the odd stray car and a few horse-riding farmers, but more often than not, the roads were deserted.

We stopped at a small country house where an old *señora* sold hand-sewn clothes. She didn't seem to notice, let alone judge the absurdity of our bathrobes, just being content to have a couple of customers so far from the city.

Maria-Carla chose some dark blue jeans and a button-up chambray shirt. A DNI agent one minute; a cowgirl the next. I went with some cargo pants and a green linen short-sleeve shirt. Camouflage, but breathable—perfect for life on the run. Outside, our driver stood in the shade, away from the burn of the afternoon sun. By the look of it, he must've smoked about five cigarettes in succession, which explained the wheezy breathing.

From a compact travel purse that'd survived both the gunfire and the underwater plunge, Maria-Carla pulled out a wad of notes and paid for the clothes.

We hit the jungle road again, passing coffee farms, tiny eateries, and bars run out of back yards or garages, bearing homemade signs reading *restaurante* or *cervecería*.

There eventually appeared a small colorful town in the distance, *un pueblo poco*, built on the edge of a deep green lake that expanded for miles.

"We're here," said Maria-Carla.

"Where?"

She smiled. "La Pequeña Montaña. My hometown."

The Little Mountain.

We crossed an old bridge into a maze of colonial townhouses, each one painted in different colors, similar but unique, like novels on display in a bookstore window. There were yellow window frames, deep-red balconies, and sunset-pink rooftops. The pavements were carved with patterns, and the concrete walls were splashed with character art. Painted on one was *The Pink Panther*, leaning back, grinning out to the world. His sleepy eyes seemed to watch us as we rolled by. Maybe he came alive when the sun went down?

Despite the gravity of the situation, it felt all right to be a tourist for a moment. And hell, three years of artistic failure behind me and a deadly mission ahead, you could argue a vacation was deserved.

Maria-Carla seemed lost in time at each passing sight. I supposed there was a memory every way she looked.

"You alright?" I asked.

"Yes. It's just strange to see my home after so long."

"I guess it's been a while?"

"So long that I didn't know if I would ever return."

The taxi wobbled its way through the cobblestone streets, passing coffee shops, fruit stalls, and flower stands packing up for the evening. End of the business day in La Pequeña Montaña.

Finally, we circled a roundabout, slowing before a two-story building painted in purple and gold. Outside, a tattered sign read *El Jaguar Cantante: Bar y Restaurante.*

The Singing Jaguar.

"*Aquí, por favor,*" said Maria-Carla.

The driver let us out, u-turned, and departed, looking grateful to be let off alive.

Maria-Carla studied the old bar before us with shimmering eyes, preparing herself. She approached the door and went inside.

The place had a rustic ambience. Faded purple walls. Small wooden tables. The kind of haunt where a young couple would go to share their first dance, and an old couple would go to relive it. On a one-step stage in the left corner was a microphone stand, and painted on the wall behind, was a jaguar, crouched low with its tail high, like it could leap from the wall any second.

"*Lo siento, estamos cerrados,*" called a voice.

Sorry, we are closed.

The voice belonged to a squat older woman in an apron, sweeping behind a bar with a broom about as tall as she was.

"*¿Gloria?*" asked Maria-Carla.

The woman behind the bar looked up, froze, and just about dropped the towering broom.

"*Maria-Carla... ¿Eres tú?*"

The woman carefully came around the bar, like one wrong move and the ghost before her would disappear.

"*Soy yo, Gloria,*" said Maria-Carla.

The two women were just an arm's length from one another.

Gloria shook her head. "*Dijeron que eras—*"

They said you were—

"*Lo sé,*" said Maria-Carla.

I know.

Gloria stepped closer, and they shared a tight, reunited embrace. As I stood by, I felt like exactly who I was—some random guy off to the side with no place in the moment.

Maria-Carla turned to me. "Lou, this is Gloria. She was a friend of my mother. *Gloria, este es Lou.*"

She paused, clearly a little unsure of how the hell to introduce me. Hell, I wouldn't have known either. "*El es alguien en quien confió,*" she said at last.

He is someone I trust.

I kept things formal and offered my hand, but she ignored it, clasping my face and planting a kiss on my cheek.

"Then you are a good man," she said. "Because this girl never trusted anyone."

Gloria pulled out a bottle of rum and three glasses from below the bar. "Tonight, we drink."

And so we drank, 'til the sun went to bed and the moon took its turn to shine on the peaceful Colombian town. The two women spoke in Spanish far too colloquial for my *gringo* ears to keep up, but I caught the odd word or two.

Above the bar was a framed photo of a couple who looked to be in their late forties. The man had wavy hair and kind eyes. He looked into the camera with a contagious smile, like he'd cracked a joke right before the click of the camera. The woman had long dark hair, high cheekbones, and the same almond eyes as Maria-Carla.

Gloria noticed me studying the image, then nodded to Maria-Carla. "She took that photo, you know."

Maria-Carla smiled faintly. "I remember like it was yesterday."

Abruptly, she stood and excused herself to the bathroom.

Gloria waited until Maria-Carla left, then spoke softly. "They are her parents. That photo was taken two weeks before they were killed."

"Jesus," I said. "How old was she?"

"She was seventeen. This bar belonged to her family. The three of them ran this place together."

Gloria sipped her rum, reliving the memories of a lost time.

"Her father, Tulio, was a chef, and her mother, Laura, ran the restaurant. Maria-Carla grew up working here. She would wait tables and help her father in the kitchen. But on Friday and Saturday nights, she would sing. People came from all around just to hear her voice."

I studied the stage in the corner and pictured a young Maria-Carla singing songs before the locals. She must've had every teenage boy in town drunk and crazy in adolescent love.

"Everything changed after they were killed."
I said nothing and waited for Gloria to go on.
"There was a war in this country. There still is. At the time, the paramilitary and the guerrillas were killing each other. They said it was political, but that was a lie. It was about money. They wanted control."
"Control?"
"Of the crops. One afternoon, her mother and father had visited a fruit market a few miles away. On the road back, they came across a paramilitary unit with their guns to the head of a young man they had accused of working for the guerrillas. Tulio and Laura knew this young man. He was the son of a coffee farmer who worked at the local market. He was saving money to go to university. They stopped to help, to try to convince the paramilitary to let him go. But, they didn't. *Simplemente los mataron a todos.*"
They killed them all.
"After that, Maria-Carla didn't sing anymore. She had inherited this place, but she said she could no longer stay. She gave the business to me and went away. She never said where she was going, or what she would do. That was the last time I saw her."
"I should have come back sooner," said Maria-Carla, returning. "I am so sorry, Gloria."
"I understood," said Gloria. "We all did."
Later in the evening, the town locals began to filter into the bar. One by one, they noticed the presence of the once-disappeared Maria-Carla. They soon approached to welcome her home, to tell her how she was missed or how they always believed she would one day return.
They asked no questions as to where she'd been or what had taken her away. It seemed they wished for nothing else but to celebrate the return of a girl once thought to be gone forever.
As the bar filled up, and the rum continued to be

served, the locals started to murmur in anticipation; a calling for something specific. I looked to Gloria and asked what the commotion was.

Gloria smiled in the direction of Maria-Carla. "They want her to sing once again."

27

As raindrops hit the roof like melting bullets, the show at *El Jaguar Cantante* was set to begin; a small-town bar packed to the gunwales, the locals assembled to witness the return of a ghost. Maria-Carla stepped out of the shadows and into the circle of a stage spotlight. She wore a black, off-the-shoulder dress and high heels, and the look in her eye was identical to that of the hunting jaguar frozen in time behind her.

She raised a hand to the microphone and tapped it with her finger, as if to greet an old friend for the first time in too long. Beside the stage, a man began to strum a guitar.

After the opening riff, Maria-Carla began to sing.

The crowd fell silent, captivated by the sound of her voice. I couldn't understand all the lyrics, but I believe it was about how to kill the devil.

As the song progressed, a fire emerged in Maria-Carla's voice, a rise in octave that ignited a passion amongst the onlookers. As the crescendo approached, they cheered louder, uplifted by the artistry they were hearing. When the final chorus arrived, her voice had evolved to a soulful cry.

But, on the cusp of the final note, she paused. The bar fell silent. After a moment of suspense, Maria-Carla raised a finger, cueing the guitarist. I expected a crashing finale, but instead, she let the last words escape in a whisper, accompanied only by the falling raindrops.

"Esta noche el diablo muere en el frio."

Tonight, the devil dies in the cold.

Maria-Carla stepped back from the microphone.

The whole of *El Jaguar Cantante* erupted. There were yells and whistles all around, all of us bound by this moment in time because we knew we had witnessed something extraordinary.

"*Gracias,*" said Maria-Carla.

The fight was far from over. Maria-Carla had returned to her roots, but not for good. By morning she'd be gone, off to finish what she'd started a lifetime ago.

I had glimpsed her vulnerability, but it had already disappeared. Now, the same fearless woman who had captured my heart from across a crowded ballroom, had returned.

El Flamingo had once asked me if I'd ever been in love. I said I hadn't—that I wasn't even sure what love was.

Between you and me, that had all changed tonight.

And so, once again, the story evolves. I know. It's a lot to get your head around. A mystery, a thriller, and now, a romance. At least for tonight. At least until tomorrow, which would bring the arrival of Diego Flores.

28

By midnight the bar had emptied. I helped Gloria clear the last few glasses and wipe down the tables. Throughout my creative endeavours, I, of course, had to moonlight for years in the hospitality industry of Los Angeles, finding work at a number of bars and restaurants around town. Actors: we're usually just waiters.

Maria-Carla had sung an assortment of songs across the night, taking impromptu requests from the crowd: *vallenato, cumbia, salsa.*

Meanwhile, as the only *gringo* from there to Tierra del Fuego, I held court. I fought through the endless conversations that had come my way, speaking much more Spanish than I thought I knew. My glass had been topped up at every turn and had endured enough clinks to smash it to smithereens. Nonetheless, it had remained somehow intact, seemingly tempered by each and every *salud.*

The locals had assumed that Maria-Carla and I were a romantic item, and I, of course, had failed to correct them. Sometimes, you just gotta smile and nod, calm, coy, and in control. Everyone will think you've got the secret to the universe written in your wallet.

After the patrons had cleared out and gone home, Gloria came toward me and studied my face.

"Eres un buen hombre, Lou. Puedo verlo en tus ojos."

You are a good man, Lou. I can see it in your eyes.

She gave me a kiss on the cheek and said *buenas noches.*

Gloria went to Maria-Carla and whispered something in her ear. They shot a quick glance my way, barely suppressing their high-school giggles. I looked out and away, fixing my eyes on the roof as if there was something there of the utmost interest. No one wants to be seen blushing.

Gloria embraced Maria-Carla and retired upstairs.

And there we were, Maria-Carla and I, alone in the midnight silence of the empty restaurant. Her watchful eyes wandered my way. I was more nervous now than when those bastards from earlier were firing bullets at my skull. I swallowed once and attempted to act like a normal person.

"It was a hell of a night," I said.

She leaned against the bar in no kind of hurry. "There is only one other bed here. We may have to share."

Stringing a sentence together had never seemed so challenging. Not again, I told myself. Not like last night.

"These chairs are actually quite comfortable," I blabbered. "I'm happy to pull a few together and sleep—"

"Lou. Stop talking."

I obeyed. A man can achieve so much by simply shutting the hell up.

She tilted her head toward the staircase. A subtle command. I protested not.

We climbed the spiral staircase to a door left open just enough to see the inviting glow of a candle-lit room. We crept inside like two teenagers, wide awake past curfew. A vase of roses on the bedside table gave the room a sweet floral scent. There were two more doors. One led to a connecting balcony, the other to an ensuite bathroom. Maria-Carla opened the balcony door, making way for a gentle breeze to swing inside.

"Take a seat," she said.

My only option was the queen bed, made up with white linen sheets.

I sat on the edge and tried to look nonchalant. Maria-Carla looked my way and grinned to herself. "I need to take a shower, but I won't be long."

I wouldn't be going anywhere. It would take some kind of a madman.

"Take your time."

She pulled a velvet towel from a drawer, kicked off her heels, and stepped into the bathroom. A moment later, the shower began running. It's not every night you earn an invitation into the chambers of the woman of your dreams. My head was spinning and it wasn't from the liquor. Tonight, I would refuse to be the coward who earlier lacked the *cojones* to make a move. While I would force nothing, I would indeed show her I was there for her, in whatever capacity she desired. If all she wanted was to be held 'til the break of dawn, then so it would be. But if she harboured the will to tear off my clothes and have her way with me, well, to that I would also sign my consent.

I stepped onto the balcony to take in some night air and ease my thoughts. The night was tranquil. The stars were an uncountable collection of winking diamonds. The man in the moon was as clear as I'd ever seen him, and I could swear he was grinning at me, a sneaky heads up that the moment we'd all been waiting for had arrived.

I heard Maria-Carla's voice behind me. *"¿Son hermosas, no? Las estrellas."*

They're beautiful, no? The stars.

I turned to see her standing in nothing but the velvet towel tied in a knot just above her breasts. And Christ, it wasn't a big towel either, stopping just past her hips to reveal her toned thighs. Her hair was still wet, and her skin glowed from the steam of the shower, which filtered through the room like mist on a mountain.

Such a sight makes a man forget the simplest of things.

"You are not going to say anything?" she asked.

"I'm, ah...thinking," I managed.

She stepped toward me. "You don't think the stars are beautiful?"

"After seeing you, they've slipped my mind completely."

She smiled, then stepped forward again. "We could both die tomorrow, Lou. You know that, right?"

"Indeed we could."

"How does that make you feel?"

I stood speechless.

"What does that make you want?"

A dangerous woman was hunting down an answer, and I'd be damned if I didn't give her the right one.

"If this is our last night alive," I said, "then all I want is you."

She took a final step my way. She was so close I could sense the heat radiating from her body, barely confined by the velvet towel, pulling me toward her like a steamy magnet.

"You know, you could remove this towel with just a single pull."

"Yes," I agreed. "The towel looks highly pull-able."

She leaned into me, just like she did that very first night at my bedroom door, the night we never kissed.

"Do you know what I want, Lou?"

She whispered against my neck:

"*Quiero que alejes la toalla.*"

I want you to pull the towel.

With such crystal-clear instructions, there was only one thing left for Lou Galloway to do. I placed my hand on her hip, moved it upward, then gave the towel the slightest tug. Swiftly, it fell to the floor, as soft and final as the last notes of the *Moonlight Sonata*. Gravity, here's to you.

Standing disrobed before me, she closed the distance and moved her hands to my shirt, undoing each button, until my shirt joined the towel on the ground. She pushed her breasts into my chest, our bodies compressed, her skin saying *hola* to mine. Her soft lips kissed my neck as I moved my hands from the small of her back to the back of her neck. Her breath sharpened. The goosebumps on her skin matched my own. I took a handful of her ponytail and gently pulled as she tilted her head back, allowing me to kiss each side of her neck. I turned her face toward mine, then kissed her. At last. Tender, but firm. Her tongue circled mine as our breathing accelerated.

In one motion, I lifted her naked body off the ground as she wrapped her legs around my torso. We stepped inside from the shine of the moon to the dim of the candles, then onto the bed, falling into the soft linen canvas.

She unbuttoned my jeans, pulled them off, and tossed them to the floor. Her lips moved down my body, from my neck, to my chest, to my abdomen. She kissed me all over before sitting on top of me.

I eased upward, finding my way to the heat between her legs in wholly unresisted simplicity, until it finally happened.

She began to push against me—slow, tight, and deep, while tracing her fingernails down my chest. I gripped the firm curve of her buttocks with both hands, assisting the wave-like movement.

Already I felt the wish to give up to my urgency right then and there. This would have been catastrophic; a sandstorm of shame. I had to slow down—to make this greatest delight last as long as it could.

Lou Galloway, going the extra mile. Don't call him a hero.

I lifted her off me and rolled her onto her side, kissed her neck, then pushed into her from behind. With one arm around her waist, I pulled her onto me, our fingers interlocked.

Her exhalations had evolved into soft moans, curbing the urge to moan louder. God knew we couldn't wake Gloria.

We soaked ourselves in the heat, and the sweat, and the fire, as time and again, she shook with climactic pleasure.

She lay on her back, pulled me on top of her, and

locked her ankles around me, commanding me not to stop. Until the return of the sun, I would do my best to oblige.

If this was to be my last night alive, I couldn't complain.

29

I woke up to the warmth of Maria-Carla's body curled around me, our legs interwoven, her hair sprawled across my chest. You had to wonder if any man in the cabinets of time had experienced a better *mañana*?

A lakeside breeze floated through the balcony doors, bringing the aromas of flower stalls and freshly brewed coffee, the signature scents of a Colombian morning.

We made love again before even saying a single word, lying together in a satisfied doze a long while after. Eventually, Maria-Carla rolled over and looked me over with a sleepy smile. *Bedroom Eyes 101 with Profesora Flores.*

"Good morning," she said.

"Damn right it is."

No matter what would follow today, it was all worth it. Taking down corruption could cost your life, but waking up with a naked Maria-Carla? Priceless.

"If we make it out of this alive, where will you go?" she asked.

I hadn't really thought about that since I'd become *El Flamingo*, yet I did have an inkling of where I'd head. "My dad always talked about this little town on the coast of Australia called Tin Can Bay. Maybe that's where I'll go. At least for a while."

She giggled. "Tin Can Bay?"

"*Si*. Tin Can Bay."

"I like the sound of that. Why Tin Can Bay?"

I remembered how he'd spoken of the place. "He made it sound like the most peaceful place in the world. There's a little café by the wharf, where you can watch the sunrise, and every morning, dolphins come into the shoreline."

I watched her close her eyes and imagine the scene. "Maybe it is the most peaceful place in the world," she said. "What will you do there?"

"I'll probably just take some time to think. See what happens. Maybe I'll write a novel or something."

She traced her finger down my chest. "What story will you write?"

"I'm not sure just yet," I said, summoning all the charm I had. "but maybe I'll write ours." It probably sounded corny, but it evoked a smile from her, so there you go.

We showered together and let nature take its course one last time, both of us knowing it would be our last chance to be alone together before our fates unfolded.

We put on yesterday's clothes, but Maria-Carla commented that we would find something more suitable for the day's events. I guess forestalling an assassination has a dress code.

Downstairs, Gloria had cooked up one hell of a breakfast. There were *arepas con queso*, scrambled eggs, and a bowl of *pandebonos* for something sweet. Most importantly, on the stove was a giant pot of drip-cloth coffee.

Gloria beamed and kissed us both. "*Buenos días.*"

"*Buenos días.*"

"*Como amaneces?*"

It's an affectionate way of asking, how did the sun rise for you? At the colloquialism, Maria-Carla couldn't contain her smile.

"*Muy bien.*"

"*Puedo verlo.*"

I can see that.

Again. High school girls.

The three of us tucked in, the morning breeze flowing through the windows. Maria-Carla and Gloria chatted away in Spanish, and I was fine to listen and nod along, without having to understand every word. More than anything, I was content to enjoy the simple gift of breakfast, coffee, and a beautiful woman beside me.

After the meal, Maria-Carla took me to a clothing store in the town center called simply, *Ropa Americana*. Every piece seemed to be tailor-made and one of its kind. Maria-Carla chose a split-leg, Marengo-gray dress and black heels.

"And what would *El Flamingo* wear?" she said, walking through a selection of fine suits. Her eyes passed over each one until finally halting on a pink linen, three-piece classic; four-piece, if you count the fedora. She picked it from the rack and held it up to me. "Try this on."

I put on the suit behind a changing room curtain. It was lightweight and comfortable and I felt instantly just that little bit cooler. When I stepped out, Maria-Carla looked me over. She held my gaze as she placed the fedora on my head, then kissed me once on the lips. "*El Flamingo*. I believe you are ready."

We returned to *El Jaguar Cantante*, where we met Carlos, an older town local, who had volunteered to drive us back to Cali. I'd met him briefly the night before, but he'd spent most of his time hovering around Gloria, who I guessed he had a soft spot for. By the time he arrived in his dusty truck, we were ready to roll.

It was time to say *adios* to La Pequeña Montaña.

Gloria held me by the hand and gave me a brief, definitive nod. I knew what it meant. *Look after her.* Then she took a deep breath and faced Maria-Carla.

"*Estarían orgullosos de ti,*" she said, as a tear formed in her eye.

They would be proud of you.

"*Te amo,*" said Maria-Carla.

"*Te amo.*"

"*Que Dios te proteja.*"

May God protect you.

"*El lo hará.*"

He will.

"As will I," I chipped in, with instant regret. It's sometimes best not to put yourself in the same breath as "The Big Fellah."

As we drove out of town, Maria-Carla kept her eyes on the rear view mirror until her hometown fell out of sight. A few turns later, La Pequeña Montaña was a memory. After a stretch of jungle highway, Maria-Carla's tears had dried, replaced by a resolute stare.

Everything we'd been waiting for was upon us.

A simple game of cards between two men, Diego Flores and Juan Moreno; one wanted power, the other wanted peace. There were secrets on both sides, and all was compromised.

Maria-Carla and I had only one advantage. We trusted each other. It wasn't a visible weapon, but it might have been more valuable than anything. She peered ahead to the valley that would lead us to our fates.

"It's time," she said.

"That it is."

"Remember. You are *El Flamingo*."

I tipped the fedora, just like I had when I'd seen her step onto the mansion balcony. She'd known what it meant then like she knew what it meant now—we were in this together.

Then, I did what I do best.

I fell back into character.

You heard the woman. I was *El Flamingo*.

30

Back in Cali, Carlos dropped us at a roadside service center on the outskirts of the city. We thanked him for the ride with a hug and a handshake. I wished him the best of luck with Gloria. He blushed, said *gracias,* and hit the road, merging with the flurry of evening traffic departing the city. We were to rendezvous with Erica, the suit-wearing CIA buzzcut, who would take us to meet Juan Moreno prior to the beginning of the operation.

Maria-Carla made a call to Diego from a roadside phone booth. It was the first time they'd spoken since we'd fled Cali. He would have arrived in the morning, and, knowing him, he would be obsessing over her whereabouts.

Maria-Carla listened with neither a smile nor a frown. At the end of the call, she nodded and put the phone down.

"Diego has arrived. He will be waiting for us at the discotheque."

Five minutes later, the same CIA, all-black, BMW pulled up to the curb. Erica stepped out. Different pantsuit. Same dark shades.

Before we got into the vehicle, Maria-Carla whispered, "Remember. We don't know who to trust. Don't mention the file."

The chip, I thought. The rosary beads! A queasiness shot through me. In the chaos of our dramatic escape the day before, I had left them in the hotel. How the hell was I going to tell Maria-Carla?

Erica's team drove us to the CIA safehouse where I'd been taken two days before. We were led back down the stairs, and into the interrogation room. On the same chair where I'd been tied up and interrogated, sat a shirtless Juan Moreno. There were his valiant face and earnest eyes I'd seen on camera—rallying thousands, igniting hope.

The two agency jocks taped a wire to his bare chest with lengths of black duct tape, questioning him while they worked.

"You sure you haven't let anything slip?"

"Not a word."

"No one in your security detail?"

"No one."

At first, he appeared calm. Focused. But as I got closer, I noticed a sheen of nervous sweat above his brow line and his breaths were deeper than those of a relaxed man.

"Mr. Moreno," said Erica. "You already know *Señora* Flores."

"*Señora*. The day is finally here," he said.

"After far too long," said Maria-Carla.

Erica cut back in. "This is the man who put this all together. *El Flamingo*."

Moreno studied me. I knew that if he had even a trace of doubt of my authenticity, it could shake him off his game. The appearance of confidence was an absolute necessity. "We appreciate your participation," I said. "Without you, this wouldn't be possible. Takes *cojones*."

He maintained his silence for a spell, then said. "You look like a dangerous man. You carry an air of violence."

Note to self: character work complete.

"I don't usually work with killers," he went on. "Why should I trust you?"

I looked him square in the eye and spoke truthfully. "You could say I have reassessed the meaning of my existence."

Moreno considered this and said, "You've found your true purpose."

"Something like that."

Moreno turned to Maria-Carla. "And you, *Señora*? Do you trust this man?"

"More than anyone."

He closed his eyes, inhaled deeply, and wiped the sweat from his forehead. "Then so be it."

The two jocks had completed their taping job. They stood back and admired their work as if they'd just finished a remarkable piece of sculpture.

"Remember," said one of them. "Avoid any sudden movements. It can obscure the sound quality."

"And you're sweating a lot," said the other. "Could be a problem. If you feel it slipping, go to the bathroom. Stick it back on."

Erica eyed the three of us: Maria-Carla, Juan Moreno, and the apparent *El Flamingo*.

"Remember. We'll be close by. We'll be listening and we'll be ready. You won't be alone."

"Did you not forget something, Erica?" asked Maria-Carla.

"What?"

"The codeword. If it turns to shit in there and we need to abort, we need a codeword."

"Right," said Erica, clearing her throat. "Any ideas?"

"Quixote," I said. "As in *Don Quixote de La Mancha.*"

Erica shot me a skeptical frown. "Don Quixote?"

Maria-Carla nodded. "It's Diego's favorite novel."

"Exactly. If it comes down to it, it will give us more time."

"Because he would feel compelled to offer his opinion," said Maria-Carla. "He wouldn't be able to help himself."

Juan Moreno smiled. "*Don Quixote* is also my favorite novel—if for very different reasons."

Erica shrugged. "Fine. Codeword *Quixote* it is."

Maria-Carla looked from Moreno to me. "Let's bring this bastard down."

As they drove us back to the service center, it was time to own up about the beads.

"Maria-Carla.... Try to stay calm, but it appears I don't have the chip *quite* on my person."

Her eyes flared. "What do you mean it's not *on your person?*"

"Well, you remember how, yesterday morning, Arturo came bursting into the room and told us men were coming and it was all very stressful—"

"Yes!"

"And then you told me to grab the gun—"

"Are you blaming me for this?"

"Not at all! But like I said, it was *very* stressful and—"

"Are the beads still in the hotel?" she cut in.

"Affirmative. The beads are still in the hotel."

Maria-Carla nodded, took a step away, and inhaled. Just when I thought she'd processed the setback well, she exploded into a violent stream of Spanish curse words. I stood by sheepishly, waiting for the rage wave to pass. Eventually, she took another breath and said, "We need to go back."

"I concur."

"Quiet."

Maria-Carla hailed a cab. The driver asked us where to take us.

"*La Vela de Cali.*"

Low profiles were required, so I went in alone while Maria-Carla waited at a nearby *Juan Valdez* café. Things seemed to have returned to normal since the traumatic events of the day before. I guess a hotel shooting is a bigger deal in some countries than it is in others. If it'd happened in New York or London, it would be a sealed crime scene for weeks on end. I smiled at the girl behind the reception desk, keeping it as casual as possible. Her name tag read *Ana*.

"How are you today, *señor?*"

"I'm good, *señorita*. Thank you for asking."

She did a quick once-over of my attire. I guess it's not every day they see a *gringo* prancing around in a pink suit. "I like your suit, *señor*."

"*Muchas gracias.* I work in fashion. *High* fashion."

"*Muy bien, señor.* How can I help you?"

I gave her the rundown, explaining that I had been a guest in the hotel in the last few days and had left something of extreme sentimental value behind during the flurry of gunshots the day before.

"You see, I'm just not cut out for dodging bullets," I said with an exaggerated giggle. "It was all a bit stressful."

"We certainly apologize for the inconvenience, *señor.* What was it that you lost?"

"My lucky string of prayer beads."

"I see."

"I am a man of God," I added for effect. "I never go anywhere without those beads."

"Nowhere?"

"Nowhere. In fact, everything I achieved in high fashion, I owe to those beads."

She nodded understandingly and went into the back office. A minute later, she returned with the beads in hand and a smile, saying a maid had recovered them during the morning clean. I breathed a sigh of relief.

"Thank the good Lord himself."

From nowhere screamed a voice through the lobby. "Lou Fuckin' Galloway!"

I turned to see none other than my agent, Tommy Blue, marching my way. As always, he wore a thrift-shop suit and strapped over his shoulder was an over-stuffed weekender. He was pouring with sweat and, outstretched, his palms were raised, like the whole thing was outrageous. I couldn't quite say why, but some part of me wasn't the least bit surprised. He was capable of things like this.

"Tommy, what the hell are you doing here?" I whispered through gritted teeth.

"Don't you dare, Galloway. I can't get a hold of ya' for two straight days. So what do I do? I assume the worst. I did what any great agent would do when his best actor disappears south of the border. I followed you down here! And why the hell are ya wearing a pink suit?"

The receptionist interjected. "I'm sorry, *señor*, do you know this man? He has been coming in here repeatedly for the last twenty-four hours asking if a 'Lou Galloway' has checked in. I told him we had no guest by that name. We were not sure if we should call the police."

I forced a smile. "Don't worry. He's an old friend. From high fashion."

"High fashion?" said Tommy.

"I see," she said, her concern remaining.

"He's harmless," I added. "Tommy, walk with me." I took him by the arm and led him outside. "How the hell did you find me?"

He emphatically wiped a rolling bead of sweat from his forehead. "Well, ain't that a fuckin' story! Last time I spoke to ya was two days ago. Thank Christ it was a video call! I couldn't see jack-shit except for a goddamn water fountain in a hotel lobby. So, what did I do? I Google-image-searched '*Colombian hotel with a water fountain in lobby.*' And then I scrolled, Galloway, I fuckin' scrolled!"

"Jesus. How long did that take?"

Tommy grabbed me by the collar, his voice psychotically quiet. "It took hours."

"Tommy, listen to me—"

"No, you listen to me! You made it, kid."

"What?"

"You made it! That's what I've been trying to tell ya! You got the fuckin' role."

I stepped back and looked into Tommy's freakishly intense gaze. "What role?"

"The one they went with the other guy for!"

"What happened to the other guy?"

Tommy's eyes widened with glee. "He got hit by a

unicyclist on Venice Beach! Can't walk for six weeks!
This is it, kid. The role of a lifetime."

So, the moment I'd been hoping for my entire adult
life had arrived at last. And yet, I felt nothing.

"You're the guy," Tommy continued. "I told 'em I had
to go to Colombia to track you down. Only intrigued
'em more. I told 'em, 'you know, the real actors of the
world, you can never fuckin' find 'em. They're mystical, you know, tortured artists always in search of an
escape, but—'"

"Tommy. I can't take the role."

"Excuse me?"

"I can't take the role."

"Why the hell not?"

Across the street, I saw Maria-Carla. She mouthed,
Who the hell is he?

"Tommy, today is not the day for this. We're in danger right now, and I need you to leave Colombia. Now."

"I ain't goin' nowhere. Not without you."

Maria-Carla was headed our way. "Who is this
man?" she asked.

Tommy turned to take in the sight of her for the first
time and just about went into cardiac arrest. "Holy
shit!"

"Tommy, this is Maria-Carla. Maria-Carla, this is
Tommy. He's my agent."

"Your agent?"

"Yeah," said Tommy, trying to regain his composure. "His agent. And if you think you can just waltz
over here with your dress, and your hair, and your
face, and take away my actor, you got another think
comin' lady."

Maria-Carla stepped close into his personal space—
"Stop talking."

"I'm sorry?"

"Clearly, you are a smart man. To recognize such
talent takes great instinct. I respect what you've done,

coming all the way down here. But, right now you are in danger. You need to leave. Now! Got it?"

Tommy looked like he'd had a spell put on him. "Yes ma'am," he said. "I got it."

Maria-Carla looked to me. "Did you get it?"

I held up the file. "Sure did."

She thought for a moment and asked, "Do you trust Tommy?"

I took a long hard look at my agent. A dishevelled, washed-up, L.A. hustler who'd tiptoed the fine line of failure his entire life, but had never given up on himself—or me, for that matter.

"Yeah. I trust him."

"Then give him the chip."

Tommy and I replied simultaneously. "What?"

"Tommy, Lou is going to give you a string of rosary beads. Inside these beads is an electronic chip that contains information that is very valuable."

"Valuable information," said Tommy. "God that's Hollywood."

"*Silencio*. You guard this file with your life. When you are safely back in Los Angeles, you take it to the media. Do not trust the authorities. Only the media."

"What the hell is on the file?"

"Details of Diego Flores' drug operation. And everyone involved."

"Diego Flores? The same Diego Flores on the FBI's Most Wanted List?"

"Correct."

"Holy shit this really *is* Hollywood."

Wavering for a moment, I asked Maria-Carla, "You sure you want him doing this?"

"Yes. If anything happens to us, the truth will have a chance to survive."

I gave the rosary beads to Tommy and popped open the cross for him. "That's neat," he said.

"Thank you for helping us, Tommy," said Maria-Carla.

He zipped the beads tightly into his suit jacket. "Yeah, you bet."

Maria-Carla stepped toward the road to hail a cab. Tommy turned my way and said, "I've never seen anything like her."

"You're tellin' me."

"Hey, kid. I don't blame ya. If it'd been me with her, I woulda' stayed too."

"Easy, Tommy."

Tommy ran his hands through his hair and clasped my shoulder. "I guess we're finally doing something big, huh Lou?"

"After all these years."

He paused a moment. "What do I tell the studio?"

I smiled. "Tell them I already found it."

"You already found what?"

"The role of a lifetime."

31

By the time we arrived, the falling sun had left Cali in shadows.

Our taxi pulled up to a baroque establishment with broad stairs and high-arching doors, where a security team awaited. Two bouncers the size of linebackers stood on either side of a stone-faced redhead who looked like she'd definitely committed homicide at least once in her life.

When she spotted Maria-Carla, the redhead said something to the first man, who said something to the second. They cleared a path, and the woman stepped forward to greet her.

"Señora Flores. Tu marido te está esperando dentro."

Your husband awaits you inside.

We were led inside and down a long corridor to a stainless-steel elevator that presented our blurred reflections. The redhead pushed a button for level twenty-three, second from the top. The elevator doors opened and we stepped into a multi-floor nightclub, submerged in a dark blaze of red and purple strobe lights. Old-school funk bounced off the walls, too loud to exchange passing comments. Groups of high-rolling revelers sat in leather booths, where champagne stood in ice buckets on circular tables. Heads turned as we passed. *Who the hell is the man in the pink suit?*

We came to a cordoned-off staircase guarded by another bouncer. The redhead moved him aside with a wave of her hand and escorted us up the stairs into a private VIP room.

It was a quiet, exclusive space with its own private bar, reserved only for those with either wealth, power, or status. In the middle of the room was a poker table beneath a vintage lampshade that illuminated the brilliant green baize. Standing by was a croupier, sorting stacks of chips into even piles. His attire was a black waistcoat over a neat white shirt tucked into black slacks. As he stood outside the reach of the light, his face was concealed by shadow.

Diego Flores sat in a corner of the room in a black three-piece suit. His legs were crossed, his hands were together, and his eyes were dark stones. He didn't immediately rise to greet us, instead choosing to observe us for a moment. Resting in his lap was a liquor bottle. A gift intended for Moreno, I guessed.

"Just when I was starting to worry," he said.

He finally stood and moved toward his wife. He touched her face and said, "*Te extrañé, mi amor.*"

I missed you, my love.

"*Yo también,*" she answered. "*Con todo mi corazón.*"

With all my heart.

I noticed the bottle in Diego's hand was fully tinted, to the point you couldn't see the liquor inside. Diego shook my hand. Despite the room's warmth, his palm was cold.

"*El Flamingo.* It seems you're as good as they say."

I said nothing.

"I have to thank you," he said. "I'm told the two of you ran into trouble."

"Nothing we didn't expect."

"And you saved the love of my life, she tells me."

Of course, it'd been the other way around, but I had to play along. "The threats were handled."

"Then I hired the right man, didn't I?"

"I appreciate your words, *señor*. But the job is not yet finished."

"No. It's not."

Diego wrapped his hand around Maria-Carla's waist, who stiffened under his touch. He glanced from her to me and said, "It's been an interesting forty-eight hours, hasn't it?"

I held his gaze. "It certainly wasn't mundane."

"No sign of Arturo?" he asked.

"Not since the attack."

"My hotel staff failed to recover his body. It makes you wonder where his loyalty lay."

Diego placed his hand on my shoulder as if we had once been great comrades. "In these uncertain times, it's good to have *El Flamingo* by my side."

Before I could reply, there was a knock on the door. The redhead re-entered. "*Señor Flores*. Your guest has arrived."

Juan Moreno entered the room escorted by a three-man security detail. He was dressed in a navy suit and tie. Since I had seen him back at the safe house, he had shaved and slicked back his hair, and his tension from before seemed to have cooled. If he was still battling his nerves, he did a damn good job of hiding them. In fact, he looked like he might have just come from a successful rally, and had I not seen it being applied with my own eyes, I never would have believed he was wearing a wire. He approached Diego and stretched out an unshaking hand. "*Señor* Flores. Welcome back to Colombia."

"Always a pleasure, Mr. Moreno. Allow me to introduce you to my wife, Maria-Carla."

"*Señora Flores*," said Moreno. "*Mucho gusto*."

They exchanged a brief kiss on the cheek, playing the role of total strangers to perfection.

Diego looked over the security detail who stood behind Moreno. "I see you brought the cavalry, Mr. Moreno. While I understand the precaution, I'm almost insulted," he motioned to me, "when all I brought was a valued business associate. He flew in today from California to partake in our game. He is also a keen card player."

"Keen, yes, but highly unskilled," I interjected, offering my hand to Moreno. "While I don't follow politics, Diego tells me you're doing fine things for your city."

"And hopefully my country, one day," responded Moreno. "*¿Habla español?*"

"I'm embarrassed to admit that it's far from fluent,"
I replied. "Would it bother you to maintain our conversation in English?"

"Not at all. I'm happy for the chance to practice. In
which aspect of business do you specialize?"

I hadn't expected Moreno to request details, but I
had it covered. "I take care of the typesetting."

"Typesetting?" he replied thoughtfully. "Somewhat
of a lost art, wouldn't you agree?"

He must've been the only guy in the world who actually knew what typesetting was.

"It's certainly on its way out," I responded. "But it
remains an integral element of a number of niche business processes."

Whatever the hell I'd meant by that, Moreno acted
like he understood. "Well, it's a pleasure to meet you."

"Likewise."

We proceeded to sit at the poker table. Diego and
Moreno faced one another, staring across the green
divide. I sat between the two with a view of the entrance.
I'd once read in a spy novel to never have your back to
the door, and while you can't rely solely on fiction for all
expertise, this seemed like sound advice. Maria-Carla
sat close to Diego, maintaining proximity, but only on
the surface. I now saw her every move as the calculated
action of a character. None of it resembled the real her.

"I see you brought a bottle, Mr. Flores," said Moreno.

Diego placed the bottle on the poker table. "It is my
gift to you. A fine mezcal, for after our game."

"*Muchas gracias*, Mr. Flores. I look forward to shar-
ing it with you."

The redhead, now adopting the role of *maître'd*,
asked what she could get us to drink. Diego requested
a rum for himself and pinot noir for Maria-Carla.
Moreno asked for a cerveza.

"Make it two," I said. "Anything stronger and I'll
start playing *Snap*."

As my joke crashed and burned, Diego interlaced his fingers and smiled at Moreno.

"Dealer," he said. "Whenever you're ready."

The croupier began to shuffle the cards, and said, "Gentlemen. Let's begin."

When he spoke, I had to fight not to gasp with surprise. The croupier's voice was one I'd heard before, on the day I found myself at that lonesome coastline bar in Mexico, the same voice of gravel and time that belonged to the stranger who'd appeared at my side as the sun went down. It was the man who sold typesetting.

The croupier stepped out of the shadows and into the light.

One by one, he locked eyes with each of us in the fashion of a consummate gentleman. When he looked my way, there was the slightest hint of a grin on his face, one that said we'd met before—that he'd been watching all along. That he'd placed a hefty bet on me, and I hadn't let him down.

Standing tall before the table, he began to deal the cards.

Maria-Carla glanced my way. In a split-second, near-telepathic conversation, using nothing but our eyes, I sought to tell her what the hell had just happened: that the real *Flamingo* had returned.

32

Down here in Colombia, they didn't play Texas Hold'em, the modern-day style of poker that dominates the casinos of Vegas. They play the original Five-card Stud, like hard-nosed outlaws in an Old West saloon.

Diego won the first hand with three jacks against Moreno's pair of kings. He scooped up the chips with feigned humility. "A lucky start," he said.

Moreno took the second hand on an empty bluff, having nothing but a pair of fours. From there, the game had seesawed, time ticking on, neither man gaining a clear advantage.

Meanwhile, I had only partaken in the occasional hand, an intentional move. Not only was it paramount that I retain the role of an observer, but I was simultaneously processing the significance of *El Flamingo*'s return.

Being the croupier, he was in control of the game, and in that sense, the entire room. Between hands, he employed trick-shuffle techniques that looked like something out of *The World Series of Poker*. He showed no sign of fatigue or loss of focus. He had remained as still and incalculably deadly as a black mamba, but as poised as, well, a flamingo.

What did his reappearance mean?

Maria-Carla was right. Clearly, he had been tracking us, monitoring us from a distance like the enigmatic mastermind his legend portrayed. It was clear that the set-up of the mistaken identity had been deliberate, not a ploy to escape. He had never abandoned me, which was something, but he *had* sent me on a path of numerous near-death encounters. If I was a cat with nine lives, I'd be cutting it fine. Whose side was he *actually* on? That was the sixty-four-thousand-dollar question.

We were around ninety minutes into the game, and the poker itself had become somewhat irrelevant. What mattered now was the game *within* the game.

I studied Moreno. A strand of finely combed hair had fallen to the side in the heat of the room, but his chin was held high, and his shoulders were back.

Diego watched Moreno closely, but appeared somewhat less engaged than his opponent. Every now and again he would break away from the cards just to observe his wife, as if she intrigued him more than the thrill of a card game.

Maria-Carla had kept her hand on Diego's back, watching him play with the appropriate adoration of a loving wife. Though she focused most of her attention on him, I noticed her eyes move from the dealer to me on several occasions, calculating, remaining alert, staying ready.

The stack of chips in the center of the table was growing, the sign of a hand getting serious. Moreno tossed in another fistful of chips.

"Raise," said Moreno.

Diego placed his cards face down on the table, pausing the hand, as if in no real hurry to finish the game. "You know," he said. "It is no surprise to see you play with such tenacity, *compadre*. After all, you are a tenacious man."

Moreno said nothing.

Diego picked up a black chip from the pot and twirled it between his fingers. "Your style of play reflects how you conduct yourself. Your career. You've proved yourself worthy in the field of politics. You stand by the values you put forth. That takes a rare kind of valor in this world of ours, don't you think?"

The real Flamingo eyed each man, the professional smile still on his face.

"Juan Moreno," continued Diego, "what is it they say about you? If I'm not mistaken, they call you 'The man with the roadmap out of corruption,' no? Wasn't that the slogan?

"Yes. That is the slogan."

"And what is corruption? What does it look like?"

Moreno joined Diego in placing his cards face down on the table. "It's not something you can often see, Diego. It is everywhere, but invisible. It hovers in the mentality of those in power, and deep within their back pockets. It is behind closed doors that are only unlocked after dark. It is beneath the floorboards like hungry snakes. It is all around us. But it's a rare thing to look it right in the eye."

Moreno stared at Diego, then said, "I believe it is your play."

Diego smiled. "I haven't forgotten. I'm simply enjoying the search for your tell. For me, it is the best part of the game."

Diego broke his glance from Moreno and turned to me. "You know, I've wanted to do business with Mr. Moreno for a long time, but it seems to be a wasted pursuit. He refuses to meet me halfway. It makes me wonder, what makes him tick?"

There was an uncomfortable wave of silence before Moreno said, "I can see *your* tell, Diego."

"And what is my tell, my friend?"

"It is not a twitch of the hand, a brush of the hair, or a scratch of the chin. It is the constant state of your eyes. They are empty."

The smile on Diego's face fell away. "And what has that got to do with the cards in my hand?"

"It's not about the cards in your hand. It's about who you are—who you are beneath it all."

"And who is that?"

"You are a man who has nothing."

"A man who has nothing," Diego quietly repeated to himself.

"Or maybe you are what they say you are—a vulture."

Diego became as still as the first time I saw him, staring into the desert night. "I did not create this world. I am just a product of it. The American demand creates men like me. And if it was not me who you condemn as the villain, it would be someone else. Do not blame the vulture for the killing. It did not spill the blood. It simply knew it was to be expected."

Moreno said nothing.

"Poker is an interesting game," continued Diego. "It all comes down to the art of misdirection; the art of the bluff. Some of which extends beyond the realm of a card game."

Diego let the silence linger, then added, "Let me be more specific. I know you have played me for a fool, my friend. But you are not the only one. Are you?"

Shit, I thought. He knows I'm not the real *Flamingo*. But when his gaze slithered in the direction of Maria-Carla, a chill shot through me.

He wasn't talking about me.

He was talking about *her*.

Maria-Carla returned his stare, the practiced warmth in her eyes replaced with ice. After twenty years, Maria-Carla was breaking character.

Before I could interject the designated code word, Moreno leaned forward, and said, "I can't help but be reminded of Cervantes' *Don Quixote de La Mancha*. Are you familiar with the story, Diego?"

Diego leaned back and studied Moreno, as if things had finally gotten interesting. "It happens to be a favorite work of mine," said Diego.

With the mission collapsing before our eyes, the hope was that the code word would work on two levels—to get the CIA off its ass, and to sufficiently divert Diego until they arrived.

"Mine too," said Moreno.

"Then you know Don Quixote was the greatest fool in all of literature. The old man who tried to save chivalry, who attempted to seek out evil and challenge it to a duel, living under the delusion he could right the world's wrongs and damn the inevitable. All by himself."

"But he wasn't all by himself, Diego."

"My mistake. He did have little Sancho."

Time was ticking. Where the hell was the CIA?

Moreno calmly sipped his beer, then said, "I think you may have rushed your interpretation."

"My interpretation?"

"Of the novel," said Moreno.

"Then please educate me, my friend."

"I don't think the story was as cynical as you consider. It simply posed a question."

"The question being?"

"Did the world make a fool out of Don Quixote, or did Don Quixote make a fool out of the world?'"

It was a smart move, to play to Diego's ego, luring him into the intellectual duel.

Diego smirked. "Did you forget he perished in the end? Did you forget he concedes himself a fool? That he renounces his pursuit of justice as a path of stupidity? What does that tell you?"

"That the world broke his heart, yes," answered Moreno. "And maybe that broken heart caused his death, but there lies the irony. Four hundred years later, we all still mourn the loss of *Don Quixote de La Mancha*. So what does that tell *you*, Diego?"

"I don't know. What does it tell me?"

"It tells you that without the Don Quixotes of the world, there would be nothing left to save. In fact, these Don Quixotes, these fools, are our only hope."

"Bravo, my friend," said Diego. "Quite the analysis. I'm impressed. You speak as well as advertised. I can see why they follow you with such loyalty—such gusto."

A sinister smile came over his face. "But there is no Don Quixote to save you today."

Diego brought his hands together. "I know the truth, *compadre*. It was a fine attempt, but you forgot something important about this world of ours."

"What's that?"

"Everyone works for me."

Silence engulfed the room as it seemed the worst-case scenario was now all but confirmed: the CIA had sold us out. Moreno's security detail no longer looked like protective guards, but like evil giants enclosing him. They, too, had betrayed him. Diego's earlier protection squad now entered the room, led by the stone-faced redhead. I just *knew* she was bad. They had guns and left us substantially outnumbered.

El Flamingo gave me a nod. *Stay calm.*

Moreno looked around and considered his circumstance with stoic dignity. "I had a feeling it would turn out this way."

"You were bound to lose," said Diego.

"Maybe. But I was always going to fight."

"*La verdad*," said Diego.

The truth.

"I expected this from you, Moreno. And for that, you have my respect. No one can call you a coward." Then he faced Maria-Carla and said, "But it was you who surprised me the most, *mi amor*."

He reached out and put his hand on hers. "I'm going to leave you until last." He nodded at the armed men who stood over Moreno. "Kill him."

33

The gunman directly behind Juan Moreno put his weapon to the famed politician's head, but a sudden movement to his left distracted him. It was the hand of the croupier, the hand of *El Flamingo*, flamboyantly trick-shuffling the cards. For a mad moment, the whole room stared. Hypnotized. Not so much as by the skill of his manipulations, but by its unexpectedness.

Then he threw the deck of cards in the air, creating a wave of confusion while keeping hold of a single card. In a lightning-fast move, he used the card to swipe the throat of the gunman, flamboyance turning into violence in less than a second. Blood spilled from the gunman's neck as he collapsed against the wall.

In the next instant, Maria-Carla stood up rapidly, upending the card table with the same motion, throwing both Moreno and me out of harm's way. She then drove the table forward, slamming it into two of Moreno's bodyguards, who were now too confused by Maria-Carla's unforeseen attack to get off a shot. The result was a train-wreck of injury: broken noses, smashed collarbones, and bruised egos.

I counted three down as I remained frozen in place, a useless spectator.

Two more charged *El Flamingo* as he reacted with a swift side-step. The deadly card still in hand, he slashed the first one's throat with an outstretched forehand. On the returning backhand, he caught the other, Federer-like in his technique. Both men fell to the floor, their throats draining. Five down. Who knew that in a simple twist of fate, a jack of hearts could be so lethal?

Across the room, Maria-Carla faced the biggest man of all—a six-foot-seventeen log of a man with no neck and a blatant history of steroid abuse. He spat out "*Vamos, puta!*" in her direction, then lined up a right hook.

Maria-Carla ducked and returned with an upper-cut to his groin. The steroid-log let out a squeal and dropped to one knee. Maria-Carla followed with a straight right to the Adam's Apple. Another one down.

El Flamingo ducked under the gunfire and drove yet another gunman all the way into a bar shelf. In a deafening crash, the entire collection of bottles came shattering down. Another one down for the count.

As chips of wood and gunsmoke blurred the air, the redhead stood with her gun pointed at Maria-Carla.

Then *El Flamingo* emerged through the haze, armed with a...*a bottle of brut champagne?* With a flick of his thumb, he popped the cork to release an explosion of carbonated alcohol right into the redhead's face. Temporarily blinded, she fired her gun way off target, the bullets ricocheting off the walls. *El Flamingo* flipped the champagne bottle to Maria-Carla who caught it in one hand and brought it down onto the redhead's skull.

Eight down. Only one to go.

Diego Flores.

Diego stood across the room, the opaque whiskey bottle suspended in his hand. Time seemed to slow as I experienced a micro-flashback to the night Diego and I had met. When I'd looked over the contents of his desktop something in particular had stood out.

Una pistola en una botella! Diego was armed, and I cursed myself for not seeing it coming.

He smashed the bottle on the edge of his seat as if he were cracking an egg.

The pistol fell to the floor. Diego picked up the weapon as the dust and gun smoke cleared. With *El Flamingo* stranded across the room, there was nothing between Maria-Carla and the aim of Diego's gun. Diego sniggered, moving as if he had all the time in the world. On the other side of the room, Maria-Carla retained the sharp, jagged neck of the smashed champagne bottle in her hand.

Diego eyed the barrel of his gun like it was his only true friend, then looked at Maria-Carla. *"Me rompiste el corazón."*

You broke my heart.

As he raised the gun, he spoke the words, *"Adios, mi amor."*

But before he could fire, Maria-Carla hurled the broken bottleneck toward Diego with ninja-like precision. There was the squelch of pierced skin, followed by a ghastly shriek from Diego. It was a hell of a shot, the jagged glass hitting him right between the eyes.

Still alive, Diego dropped to a knee. Zombie-like, he managed to wrench the glass blades from his forehead while blood leaked down his face. With his last reserve of energy, he raised the gun once more and fixed it on Maria-Carla.

No more would I stand frozen. Only one thing to do.

I charged toward the gun's line of fire.

Diego squeezed the trigger.

I dived in front of Maria-Carla.

The gun went off.

I must have hit the floor, but I felt nothing. I was a man unbound from the limitations of gravity. Had the gun misfired?

From the ground, I watched Diego collapse, hitting the floor in a lifeless heap. Although his eyes remained open, there was no doubt—Diego Flores was dead.

I tried to pick myself up, but it seemed I was pinned to the floor by some kind of astronomical weight. Maybe that bullet *had* hit after all?

My hand went instinctively to my gut, where warm liquid seeped from my stomach, almost like I'd wet myself.

I looked up to see *El Flamingo* closely instructing Juan Moreno, who gave me a stoic nod, some kind of man-to-man gratitude. He then left the room in an almighty hurry.

At last, Maria-Carla appeared at my side, wrapping her arms around my head, the tips of her hair touching my face.

"Why the hell did you do that?" she demanded. "Why didn't you just stay where you were!"

There wasn't the time to argue with her. Not at the rate I was fading. I figured I was bleeding out, and if you've ever been to the movies, you know that a gut shot never ends well.

Maria-Carla clasped my face and pressed her lips against mine, firmly, as though if she kissed me hard enough, it might stop the bleeding. I kissed her back, but only just. An all-powerful sleepiness washed over me that seemed impossible to resist. Not even the incredible scent of Maria-Carla's perfume could bring me back to life.

Though my vision was blurring, I made out *El Flamingo*. Of course, he was ripping off his shirt to bind my wound, looking like he knew just what to do in times like these. Damn him. I tried to speak, to tell him I was meeting my demise, but there was no use, and, for the love of God, could he put his damn shirt back on and quit stealing my thunder in my last moments alive. I would soon be gone, but he and Maria-Carla still had a chance to make it out alive as long as they hightailed it out of here right this minute!

As for me, I could rest easy. My legacy was complete. While I'd left L.A. a failure, I'd depart this world a legend. I'd played the role of a lifetime—"til-close-of-curtain."

Let my epitaph read: *Lou Galloway*—The greatest actor never known, lucky enough to have never made it in Hollywood.

The lights were really starting to dim. Staying awake felt like trying to stop the sun from setting.

I took a look at Maria-Carla for the very last time. God, she was beautiful. She made for one hell of a final sight. I had to admit, there were a thousand worse ways to go.

As my heart slowed to its final few beats, I remembered the words of *El Flamingo* back in Mexico. We'd talked of what it meant to be in love. I'd said I had no idea. Before he walked away, he said one last thing:

"It's knowing you'd take a bullet for them at any given moment."

Yep. It *sure* was.

If only I'd had a little more time, I would've told her that I loved her.

But hell, since the moment we'd met she'd been reading my mind. I closed my eyes with a smile. She would have already known.

34

I opened my eyes and saw my father standing over me with a hand on my shoulder, gazing ahead to some far destination. The luminous glow of the moon and stars presented him in a silhouette, obscuring his face. I knew it was him, though. I was sure of it.

I quietly said, "Hey Dad."

He looked down at me and smiled. "I got you, Lou."

He was at the wheel of what felt like a magic speedboat, guiding us over misty waters. The engine's hum was like the purr of some mystical big cat upon whose strong back we rode. Sure, it may be a wild and dangerous animal, but you somehow knew he was on your side, that this great cat would keep you safe, using his mighty power to protect you. Obviously, we were on our way to a little town called Heaven.

I was pleased that, despite my many failings, I'd done enough of the right things to warrant acceptance.

But confusion began to set in while recalling the unfolding of events until I was gunned down for good.

The game of cards.

Diego Flores.

El Flamingo.

Most importantly, *Maria-Carla*. Was she safe? Had they made it out of Cali? Sure enough, I had been a necessary casualty, but when I'd passed, they had still been alive with a fighting chance. I wanted answers and I wanted them now. My frustration built to anger, but the anger brought me back to exhaustion.

I closed my eyes for what could have been minutes, hours, or possibly days—impossible to tell when you're in a purgatorial time zone.

When I opened them again, the skies held a softer tint, filled with shades of pink and blue, similar to the morning skies back on Earth. In fact, what I was seeing bore a suspicious resemblance to a Cali sunrise.

Wait, if this was Heaven, it sure looked a lot like Colombia.

I looked at my father again. While I had before seen him so clearly, I now wasn't so sure it was him anymore.

"Dad?"

The man at the wheel turned to me. "He would have been proud, Lou."

There was something in his eyes that said I could trust him. That he was sincere. He winked, then fixed his gaze ahead. Come to think of it, he looked a hell of a lot like the man from the bar in Mexico. The man who sold typesetting. The man they called *El Flamingo*.

I exhaled painfully, trying to summon the strength to look around us, to get an idea of where the hell we were.

With my only ounce of energy, I heaved myself up with what felt like the arms of the weakest man in the world, pushing through the stabbing agony in my stomach, just enough to see over the side of the boat.

We were in the jungle, speeding across a deep-green river, camouflaged by the heights of a thousand palm trees.

My arms couldn't take any more, so I let myself fall back to the floor of the boat. In a blurry haze, I pieced things together: the pain, the river, the palm trees, and the man at the wheel who wasn't my father.

That bullet from Diego's gun hadn't taken me out.

This was not the route to Heaven.

I was still alive and still in Colombia.

35

I awoke to the crackle of burning wood. I was soaked in sweat and had a searing headache. Slowly, I inspected my whereabouts. I appeared to be in a rainforest cave, where a small campfire made dancing shapes on the jagged stone walls.

I was lying on a bed made up of leaves tossed over hard ground, my blood-stained suit jacket acting as my blanket. I sat up and felt a rip of pain in the side of my stomach, the wound tightly wrapped by a torn strip of cotton tied in a multi-faceted knot.

On the other side of the fire sat *El Flamingo*. His eyes were closed and his back was straight. He wasn't sitting cross-legged like a Shaolin monk or anything, but he was certainly in some form of zen-like meditation, in harmony with the flames before him. His waistcoat was gone, and his white shirt was now shredded and streaked with dried blood. He opened his eyes and met my gaze with an audacious grin.

"Evening, Lou."

Evening? The nerve of the man.

"Where are we?"

He let his eyes prowl the cave walls, lost in wonder. "It's a jungle cave built by the Misak people, the original tribe of the Valle de Cauca region."

I wasn't quite up for a history lesson, but I appreciated the background information. "Nice."

"I removed the bullet and treated the wound with cinnamon bark. Should be enough to get you through."

"Cinnamon bark?"

"It's old school. A jungle tactic."

The ego of the guy.

"Where are we?" I asked.

"We're about a hundred miles from Cali. We've been here for the last eight hours."

He held out a bottle of cheap mezcal, just like the

one from the beachfront bar in Mexico. "Care for a drink?"

Between the gunshot, the headache, and the colossally uncomfortable cave-floor bed, I considered a drink to be thoroughly deserved.

"Sure."

The bottle was about two-thirds full, so I guess he'd started without me. I couldn't blame him. If I'd had to sit in a cave for eight hours while some guy slept off a bullet wound, I would've started early too.

I took a hearty swig, and pretty soon the pain became a little less agonizing. I held the bottle up and noticed there was no drowned worm laying at the bottom.

"He must have escaped," said *El Flamingo*.

I looked up. "Sorry?"

"The worm. He must've found his way out."

The image of his escape filled me with a profound sense of victory. As it turned out, I had greatly underestimated the will of that little mezcal worm.

"Yeah. He must've."

"Maybe he's a *mariposa* now."

And maybe Don Quixote wasn't a fool?

"You've had a tough twenty-four, Lou. I'm proud of you."

I tossed back a little more mezcal, preparing to ask what I needed to know the most. "Is Maria-Carla safe?"

"She's safe," he said. "We made it out, Lou."

I felt my heart start to beat again, allowing myself a sigh of relief. I recalled the scene of blood and gun smoke before I'd been shot. "Did I dream it, or did you kill a bunch of guys with nothing but a jack of hearts?"

He shrugged. "I have a unique set of skills."

"No shit."

"Sadly, they're not transferrable."

"And Maria-Carla...where did she go?"

El Flamingo shook his head. "She didn't say. Once she knew I had you, there wasn't much time. We had to go in separate directions. She said there were things she needed to see to. She mentioned her daughter. Said you'd understand."

"Is that all she said?"

He paused. "She mentioned a couple of other things."

"You're killing me here."

With a grin, he said, "I thought you would appreciate a little suspense. You're an actor, right?"

"Flamingo, I won't hesitate to throw this bottle."

He laughed and put a hand to his chin. "She asked me to tell you she'd find you one day."

"Where?"

"The place where the dolphins come in. Said you'd understand that too."

After hearing that, I momentarily felt no pain at all. "She really said that, huh?"

"Yep. And by the look in her eye, I'd say she meant it."

Wouldn't that be something?

El Flamingo smiled for a time, then threw a handful of sticks into the fire. "It seems you've figured a few things out, Lou."

"You mean whatever the hell just happened over the last four days?"

"More or less."

"Well, you sure as shit don't sell typesetting."

"No, I don't."

For some reason, I again sensed the presence of my father. "You know, for a while there, I thought you'd abandoned me."

He gazed at me through the campfire flames, a shine in his eyes. "I was always watching, Lou. From a distance."

He swigged from the mezcal, then said, "I'd say it's about time I level with you."

36

I listened to his denouement, told over the crackling of the flames. Despite my weakened state, the gravitas with which he recounted his narrative engaged me enough to distract me almost entirely from the pain of the bullet wound.

"A long time ago, before I was known as *El Flamingo*, I was just another soldier, fighting wars in faraway lands. The agency recruited me into a classified black ops program, where they took away my identity and gave me a new name."

"*Operative 81*," I said.

"They broke me down, built me back up, and molded me into a weapon. I spent three years undercover. My mission was to find out how deep the dirt ran."

"And what did you find?"

"That this business cannot operate the way it does without many corrupt minds across multiple borders. I developed leads. I gathered intel. I made real progress. But the operation collapsed."

"You were sold out."

"All thanks to one man in the shadows making deals in the dark. By the time I identified the leak, it was too late."

Outside, somewhere in the night, a bird called through the valley. Morning was on its way.

"I was aboard a vessel moving arms into Colombia through the Caribbean coast. The men in charge of that operation had been tipped off. They knew I was working deep cover. They were gonna put a bullet in me then and there."

He left me hanging with a dramatic pause. "So? What did you do?"

"I jumped the hell overboard. They figured me a goner. How could a man possibly survive out there? But, I had one advantage. It happened to be sunset right when I jumped, and the thing about the sun is that it always sinks in the west. So, west I swam, knowing it would eventually take me to land."

I recalled our first conversation. "That was the sunset that saved your life."

"Told you it was a long story."

"And once it got dark?"

"I used the stars. They've got a way of guiding you."

The bird called again. *El Flamingo* looked in its direction, then turned back to the fire.

"So you made it to the coast?"

"Negative. But I reached somewhere else. The surrounding waters of a little island called San Andrés."

"I know San Andrés," I said. "Well, I've seen it on postcards."

"You're interrupting the rhythm of my story."

"I'm sorry. Please go on."

"In the middle of the night, exhausted and dehydrated, about ten minutes from a deep blue grave, I glimpsed a single light on the water. I called out with my last bit of energy, then blacked out."

He paused as if the story could well have ended there. "And?"

"I woke the next morning in an oceanside bedroom with a view of the whitest sand in the world. Standing over me was this woman, this *beautiful* woman. She put a cool hand on my forehead. And you know what she gave me?"

"I don't know. A warm kiss that welcomed you to life anew?"

"No, Lou. Christ's sake. I'd just met her. She gave me a chilled, green coconut. I drank every drop. I looked into her eyes—and that was it."

"*What* was it?"

"I fell in love. Guilty as charged. Never felt anything like it."

Here was the human apex of the tough, dangerous,

battle-hardened man; unkillable and fazed by nothing. Except, apparently, exposure to the unstoppable grasp of love. After the astounding violence of the day before, it was pleasant to hear such a wholesome tale.

"Her name was Esmeralda. She owned a little bed and breakfast on the island. She was a painter. The only reason she was out on the water that night was to sketch the galaxy. She told me that the moon and stars never shine as bright as when you're out at sea. It was those same stars that led me to her. Romantic, right?"

There was a lump in my throat, but don't you go thinking I shed any tears.

"Incredibly romantic."

"If she hadn't been out on the water, I would have been some shark's next protein snack."

"Serendipitous."

"Damn right it was. Over the next few weeks, she nursed me back to health, and, well, they were the happiest days of my life."

His smile began to fade. "But, at that time I lacked the wisdom to let go of who I was."

"And that's when you became *El Flamingo*?"

"To the world, I was a dead man, and dead men are untraceable. I had the knowledge and the skills to reach anyone, and they would never see me coming. I started with the man who sold me out."

He stared into the flames, his hand tightly gripping the neck of the bottle.

"I was angry, and I was dangerous. I wanted to hunt down every corrupt son-of-a-bitch I could find: the traffickers, the profiteers, the dealers, the extortionists, the killers. I couldn't let go. So I left Esmeralda and I went searching for vengeance. Worst choice I ever made."

I said nothing, allowing him the moment of regret. I'd sure as shit had a few of those myself.

"I anticipated that Flores would hire me for the

Moreno job, and I knew it was a chance to do things differently. I'd killed a lot of bad men, but I'd never saved
a good one. Here was a guy, Juan Moreno, fighting for
real change in the world. Not from the shadows, like
me, but out in the open, far braver than I would ever
be. If I could save his life, I could disappear. Become
someone else. Take my last shot at love. Like you told
me in Mexico, to go win her back."

Lou Galloway: life coach.

"Thing was, I couldn't do it alone. To save Moreno,
a lot of things had to go right. I knew I could trust
Maria-Carla. She was one of the good ones—gave her
soul to the job. But I had to find a way to reach out to
her, and to her only. I managed to get a letter to a DNI
safe house, proposing a way we could save Moreno and
bring down Flores at the same time."

"The file," I said.

"There was always a high chance the mission would
be corrupted. The file was our insurance."

"And if you were anticipating a collapse, you needed
a bird's eye view."

"That's where you came in. I needed a double. A *great*
double. This required an expert actor. A man with the
rare ability to capture the essence of another human
being. And not just any human being, a legend."

Again, the ego on this guy.

He swigged back the final few drops of mezcal. "So,
you became *El Flamingo*. Best acting I've ever seen."

I accepted the compliment in silence as I watched
the fire burn to small embers in a bed of black ash.

"It was one hell of a show, Lou. I saw it all. I was
among the dancing guests at the wedding. I was the
pilot who flew you to Cali. I even saw you salsa with
Maria-Carla. Not bad."

I remembered the shadow in the far corner of the rainforest salsa bar. Everything that was said about him
had all been true. He was one stealthy son-of-a-bitch.

"Let me guess. You were the bell boy who saved our asses with that luggage trolley."

"Close call."

"Thanks for that."

"I'd gotten you into a lotta trouble. It was the least I could do."

"Finally, you were the croupier in the game of cards."

"By then, I knew Diego had the upper hand. His drug money had purchased the revelation of Maria-Carla's undercover identity. After that, he became the most dangerous thing in the world. A heartbroken man with nothing to lose."

"How did you find out that Diego knew?"

"I had eyes on him."

Nobody ever wants to elaborate. "Eyes?"

"An inside man."

Jesus. Every man and his dog. Out with it!

"Who?"

He couldn't suppress a sly grin. "I'll give you a clue. He's a big Juan Gabriel fan."

The revelation hit me about as hard as the damn bullet. "*Arturo?*"

"That's right," he said. "He knows his stuff."

"Hold on! So, back in Mexico, Arturo knew I wasn't the real Flamingo?"

"The whole time. He was, whuddaya call it? Acting."

"No way."

"Way," he said. "He and I go back a long time."

"So, he's alive?"

"Of course. Believe me, that chubby little fellah is even harder to kill than I am."

Now that he said it, it made sense. Arturo *was* the kind of guy who could flounder his way through a hail of bullets, only to somehow tiptoe around every last one of them.

I considered how *El Flamingo* had managed to execute his audacious plan. For it to work, it had required

a puzzle of moving pieces to fit together in exactly the
right places, at exactly the right time. Only one major
question was yet to be answered.

"How did you know I would go along with it all? That
I wouldn't run?"

He gave me a thoughtful grin, seeming to search for
the right words. "I recognized something in you. I saw
you were searching for the same thing I was."

"Which was what?"

"Purpose."

The final embers of fire had fizzled out, reminding
me of the Mexican sundown we'd watched at the tiki
bar. Finality looms, but if you wait it out, there might
just be another beginning. I wondered what would be
next for *El Flamingo*.

"So, this Esmeralda," I said. "Where did you leave it
with her?"

"Last time I saw her, she was walking away from
me on a San Andrés beach. She said she wouldn't be
held in the arms of a killer. Said she never wanted to
see me again."

"Shit. You think she meant it?"

"Hard to say. She seemed pretty certain."

I wanted to provide some kind of support, but I
couldn't come up with much. "I heard women love a
man who's capable of change," I offered. "That might
get you a foot back in the door."

"I've heard that too," he said. "You can always hope."

We shared a spell of thoughtful silence before *El
Flamingo* glanced at his watch.

"Nearly six. What do you say we watch the sunrise?"

He helped me up from the bed of leaves and let me
lean on him. If it wasn't that I was well past the point
of tipsiness, walking would have been unbearable. We
saw only a black void until, at last, the gentle tips of
a newborn sun emerged from behind the curves of the
jungle mountains. In slow motion, it rose into the sky

and drove out the dark; the changing of the guard. Now we could see the beauty of the whole valley, a vast expanse of infinite green. Never before had I seen a sight so full of life.

"Hell of a sunrise," said *El Flamingo.*

At that, I had to smile. "Well, it's on its way up."

37

Soon after sunrise came the chuff of an approaching helicopter soaring out of the newly lit sky.

"Here's your ride, Lou," said *El Flamingo*.

He braced an arm around my back, holding me upright. The bullet wound still felt like hell, but my heart was beating. Maybe it was the mezcal, but it seemed I'd really turned a corner.

I took a last look at the burnt-out campfire. Every bit of the conversation we shared would remain in my heart forever. It had given me some closure—not only to the wild events of the past four days, but to something I'd been chasing for a much longer time.

A dark-green, retrograde military helicopter descended onto a patch of riverside grass, the *wop-wop-wop* of the rotors surely pissing off any nearby jaguar who'd planned a sleep-in.

Setting her down was Arturo, looking every part the pilot. Black aviators. Heroic gaze. Moustache as thick as ever. He gave me his broad smile and signature thumbs-up.

El Flamingo put a hand on my shoulder and yelled over the noise of the rotors. "He'll explain it all!"

"What about you?" I yelled back. "You're coming with us, right?"

He shook his head. "I'm going the other way, Lou. To San Andrés!"

"How're you getting there?"

"I've still got the boat."

I saw the rich-red speedboat, waiting by the river. "Gonna be a long ride," I shouted.

"Damn right. But I need time to think of what I'm gonna say. To Esmeralda."

"You'll think of something. Just don't mention type-setting!"

We burst into laughter, before a heaviness came into my chest. "So this is *adios?*"

"For now. But I'm sure I'll see you down the road."

"Thanks for believing in me," I said.

"You were a safe bet, Lou. You just *might* be the best actor in the world."

He put on his shades, then hugged me hard, how a father hugs a son when there's no telling the next time he'll be seeing him. He hoisted me into the chopper, as Arturo helped fasten me into the co-pilot's seat. Adrenaline gave me the strength to push past the pain.

Once buckled up, Arturo handed me a pair of earphones.

"*Listo?*" he asked.

Ready?

"*Listo.*"

El Flamingo stood back from the chopper, shouted something, and saluted. I returned the gesture with a tear in my eye.

We ascended from the Valle de Cauca, then headed west, following the jungle 'til the blue of the Pacific Ocean.

As we'd flown out of sight, I'd looked back at *El Flamingo*, watching him until he became a silhouette, just like the first time I saw him.

I considered what he might've said as we'd flown away. Although I hadn't quite caught it, I'm pretty sure he'd yelled:

"We did it, Lou!"

38

I looked out to the ocean from the seaside cafe and sipped from my usual—a double-shot espresso, with a jug of hot water on the side. Just like me, the coffee beans had made it all the way here from Colombia.

The sun had just risen, and I still had another hour before the dolphins would come to feed. Aside from the barista, there wasn't a soul around. This was Australia, but the sand was the same soft blend of gold and white as back in Mexico. Faraway Mexico, where I'd once ordered a cheap mezcal.

It'd been just over a year since it all happened, and still, the surrealism hadn't worn off. In fact, part of me still believed I had dreamt the whole thing, like the final spin of an eighties adventure flick that plays the audience for a fool and has them wanting their money back. Maybe I would wake any moment, back at the tiki bar, drunk and depressed, the man in typesetting nothing but a figment of my imagination.

But nope. Here I was, alive, with a bullet-wound scar to prove it.

So, how did I get from there to here?

Well, Arturo flew me out to where the edge of Colombia meets the ocean, then we traced the coastline up to somewhere in the Gulf of Panama. There, Arturo dropped me on a cargo ship captained by a guy who owed *El Flamingo* a favor. Arturo farewelled me with an incredibly convincing passport and two thousand dollars in cash. Onboard was a medic who stitched up what was finally determined to be a flesh wound and knew not to ask questions.

The cargo ship was heading for the Pacific Islands.

After a choppy, two-week journey, they'd dropped me off in Suva, Fiji.

From Suva, I boarded a flight with a sub-ideal charter that should've been called *Turbulent Airlines*. After a shaky takeoff and a dodgy landing, I arrived in Sydney. From there, I took a connecting flight to Brisbane, and from Brisbane, I boarded a tourist bus that ran up the coastline of Queensland. Fortunately, no Barb from Texas this time.

When the bus came to a fading sign that said, "*Welcome to Tin Can Bay, where the sun comes up with a smile*," I signaled the driver to let me off.

On the noticeboard of a little supermarket, I'd found a good deal on an apartment just a couple of streets back from the beach.

A few weeks after I'd settled in, an international news alert appeared on my phone:

"*Mystery file leads to break in multinational drug and arms operation.*"

The story told of hundreds of traffickers, politicians, military, and police personnel who had been arrested and charged. Shipments of drugs and weapons had been seized on just about every continent that had all been traced back to the same origin.

"*Though we still have a long way to go, this is the greatest strike at the heart of corruption so far,*" said Colombia's new president, Juan Moreno.

The article mentioned an anonymous source believed to have supplied the file who claimed he came across it by a chance encounter and gave no further details than "Leave me the hell outta this. I'm in the movie business."

Classic Tommy.

Not a day went by that I didn't think of Maria-Carla.

I would see her everywhere, only to be mistaken time after time: a woman at the market browsing the stalls among the town crowd; a dark-haired beauty reading in the far corner of a coffee shop; the shape of a feminine wanderer strolling alone at the opposite end of the beach. None would ever turn out to be her.

It began to drive me crazy. I thought I would never see her again. I really just wanted to know she was okay—that she was alive—that there was a little hope, a little *esperanza,* on the horizon.

If it had to be, I guess I could live in Tin Can Bay for the rest of my life; to wait, just in case she ever did come to town on one fine day.

I finished my coffee, paid the bill, and returned to my apartment, a cozy one-bedroom with a small kitchen having French doors that opened to an ocean breeze.

It was half an hour until the dolphins fed, so, as I did most days, I had some time to cook up some *arepas con huevos y queso. Desayuno,* as they say in Spanish.

I prepared the dough of white corn flour and water, hand-molded them into circles the size of small pancakes, crammed the middle with grated cheese, and fried them in a pan, one by one. Once prepared, I topped them with scrambled eggs and a little *salsa picante.* On the side, I had papaya, peeled and cut up into slices. Breakfast for one with the tip of my hat to Latin America.

I went to take a bite when, out of nowhere, I caught a scent of vanilla and roses, blown in by the breeze. It was as if Maria-Carla had *just* passed by the French doors. Surely, it was my scoundrel of an imagination. Maybe I'd lost it for good. A man without his mind, fallen from the sane train, tumbling down the hill of full-blown *loco.*

Do *not* believe it, Lou. It'll only break your heart.

But then, I heard three knocks on the door. They were just like the knocks I'd heard that night in Mexico when I lay in the corner suite of Diego's mansion.

Okay, universe. You got me. I'll play victim to your cruel tease one last time.

With my heart running sprints and my breath escaping, I opened the door.

Against all odds in the galaxy, there she stood.

She wore a crème linen dress, her hair to her waist, her smile a gift I could never deserve. The cover girl of the rest of my life. In my doorway stood the one, the only, gun-blazingly beautiful, *Maria-Carla Flores.*

I wanted to stand there forever, just to behold the sight of her—to press pause on perfection. But, as Arturo said on that fateful night on the coast of Mexico—*"time is of the essence."*

"If you're looking for *El Flamingo,*" I said. "He's not here right now."

She stepped a little closer. "Actually, I was looking for a man named Galloway. Lou Galloway."

"And how might this Lou Galloway be of service?"

She closed the distance between us. "I was told he could take me to see the dolphins."

I took one last second to enjoy this moment. Not the end, but the beginning—that part of the journey where it all lies ahead. I checked my watch and smiled.

"You're just in time."

Acknowledgements

I would first like to thank the nations of Colombia and Mexico, whose charm and spirit inspired a world in which Lou Galloway could adventure.

To the readership of *The Lost Gringo Chronicles*, your words and loyalty gave me a certainty of belief that, in this day and age, there are still those who value written stories, and that somehow you had the time to read mine.

To Kobe, whom I imagine would say, "rise with the sun and write till it sinks."

To the beautiful Miriam, who gifted me a commissioned painting of a poised flamingo when feelings of doubt had flooded my mind.

To my friend, Scotty Dawe, who always checked in to ask how the book was going, and called me the day he finished reading the very first draft. Luckily, it was not to say it was a piece of shit.

To my friend and creative partner, Tommy Newman, an acting genius, who taught me what it really means to be an actor, which forms the soul of this novel. Thanks for all the words of support, kid.

The world is full of lost dreamers, many with none who believe in them. For me, that will never be the case, and that's because of my family. I want to thank my brother, and best friend, Rhys Davies, who answered every call, talked me through rage and frustration, helped soundboard plot lines, hash out characters, and investigate the daunting task of promoting a book in today's day and age. Not once did you ever sound tired of helping me. To my dad, Geoff Davies, who has a hell of a lot in common with this *El Flamingo* character— and not just in terms of his past career in typesetting. You provided me with not only the wisdom of an editor's eye, but the strength of a father's support, something many struggling creatives will never have. I couldn't have done it without both of those things, Dad. Finally, to my mum, Louise Davies. I called her on the phone late one night in 2018 from downtown Auckland, telling her about a character named Lou Galloway, a failed actor who gets mistaken for an assassin and ends up bringing down a drug empire. Despite the sheer madness of it, she saw Galloway and his universe as clearly from the very beginning as I had. It meant that I never really wrote this alone. Four years, and about a hundred drafts later, she shared every page of this story with me. Without your support, Mum, there would be no book to hold. With that said, the first physical copy to be printed and bound belongs to you.

Along the way, I learned that it's not about the final product. It's about the heart of the story and the journey to tell it. This book took me around the world, from Los Angeles to Colombia, chasing the ghost of Lou Galloway, who had blazed a trail out of my imagination, into the world, and onto a printed page. So if I don't sell a single copy, nothing is lost.

It was the ride of a lifetime.

About the Author

Nick Davies is an actor-turned-writer from Wellington, New Zealand. He has appeared internationally in both film and TV. He has written short films, plays, and a collection of travel stories titled *The Lost Gringo Chronicles*.

At age twenty-seven, he took a break from acting and bought a plane ticket to Colombia to research and write his debut novel, *El Flamingo*. When not in his homeland, he can be found somewhere in Latin America, sipping a coffee or chasing a sunset, always on the search for a story to tell.

CPSIA information can be obtained
at www.ICGtesting.com
Printed in the USA
BVHW031021060323
659766BV00003B/111